D1193772

FLOWERING JUDAS

This collection contains all of the stories which appeared in the original limited edition of *Flowering Judas and Other Stories*, together with four new stories, "Theft," "That Tree," "The Cracked Looking-Glass," and "Hacienda."

Flowering Judas

AND OTHER STORIES

BY KATHERINE ANNE PORTER

HARCOURT, BRACE & WORLD, INC.

NEW YORK

Contents

Contents

MARIA CONCEPCION

María Concepción

MARIA CONCEPCION walked carefully, keeping to the middle of the white dusty road, where the maguey thorns and the treacherous curved spines of organ cactus had not gathered so profusely. She would have enjoyed resting for a moment in the dark shade by the roadside, but she had no time to waste drawing cactus needles from her feet. Juan and his chief would be waiting for their food in the damp trenches of the buried city.

She carried about a dozen living fowls slung over her right shoulder, their feet fastened together. Half of them fell upon the flat of her back, the balance dangled uneasily over her breast. They wriggled their benumbed and swollen legs against her neck, they twisted their stupefied eyes and peered into her face inquiringly. She did not see them or think of them. Her left arm was tired with the weight of the food basket, and she was hungry after her long morning's work.

Her straight back outlined itself strongly under her clean bright blue cotton rebozo. Instinctive serenity softened her black eyes, shaped like almonds, set far apart, and tilted a bit endwise. She walked with the free, natural, guarded ease of the primitive woman carrying an unborn child. The shape of her body was easy, the swelling life was not a distortion, but the right inevitable proportions of a woman. She was entirely contented. Her husband was at work and she was on her way to market to sell her fowls.

Her small house sat half-way up a shallow hill, under a clump of pepper-trees, a wall of organ cactus enclosing it on the side nearest to the road. Now she came down into the valley, divided by the narrow spring, and crossed a bridge of loose stones near the hut where María Rosa the beekeeper lived with her old godmother, Lupe the medicine woman. María Concepción had no faith in the charred owl bones, the singed rabbit fur, the cat entrails, the messes and ointments sold by Lupe to the ailing of the village. She was a good Christian, and drank simple herb teas for headache and stomachache, or bought her remedies bottled, with printed directions that she could not read, at the drugstore near the city market, where she went almost daily. But she often bought a jar of honey from young María Rosa, a pretty, shy child only fifteen years old.

María Concepción and her husband, Juan Villegas, were each a little past their eighteenth year. She had a good reputation with the neighbors as an energetic re-

ligious woman who could drive a bargain to the end.
It was commonly known that if she wished to buy a
new rebozo for herself or a shirt for Juan, she could
bring out a sack of hard silver coins for the purpose.

She had paid for the license, nearly a year ago, the
potent bit of stamped paper which permits people to
be married in the church. She had given money to the
priest before she and Juan walked together up to the
altar the Monday after Holy Week. It had been the
adventure of the villagers to go, three Sundays one after
another, to hear the banns called by the priest for Juan
de Dios Villegas and María Concepción Manríquez, who
were actually getting married in the church, instead of
behind it, which was the usual custom, less expensive,
and as binding as any other ceremony. But María Concepción was always as proud as if she owned a hacienda.

She paused on the bridge and dabbled her feet in the
water, her eyes resting themselves from the sun-rays
in a fixed gaze to the far-off mountains, deeply blue
under their hanging drift of clouds. It came to her that
she would like a fresh crust of honey. The delicious
aroma of bees, their slow thrilling hum, awakened a
pleasant desire for a flake of sweetness in her mouth.

"If I do not eat it now, I shall mark my child," she
thought, peering through the crevices in the thick hedge

of cactus that sheered up nakedly, like bared knife blades set protectingly around the small clearing. The place was so silent she doubted if María Rosa and Lupe were at home.

The leaning jacal of dried rush-withes and corn sheaves, bound to tall saplings thrust into the earth, roofed with yellowed maguey leaves flattened and over-lapping like shingles, hunched drowsy and fragrant in the warmth of noonday. The hives, similarly made, were scattered towards the back of the clearing, like small mounds of clean vegetable refuse. Over each mound there hung a dusty golden shimmer of bees.

A light gay scream of laughter rose from behind the hut; a man's short laugh joined in. "Ah, hahahaha!" went the voices together high and low, like a song.

"So María Rosa has a man!" María Concepción stopped short, smiling, shifted her burden slightly, and bent forward shading her eyes to see more clearly through the spaces of the hedge.

María Rosa ran, dodging between beehives, parting two stunted jasmine bushes as she came, lifting her knees in swift leaps, looking over her shoulder and laughing in a quivering, excited way. A heavy jar, swung to her wrist by the handle, knocked against her thighs as she ran. Her toes pushed up sudden spurts of dust, her half-

6

raveled braids showered around her shoulders in long crinkled wisps.

Juan Villegas ran after her, also laughing strangely, his teeth set, both rows gleaming behind the small soft black beard growing sparsely on his lips, his chin, leaving his brown cheeks girl-smooth. When he seized her, he clenched so hard her chemise gave way and ripped from her shoulder. She stopped laughing at this, pushed him away and stood silent, trying to pull up the torn sleeve with one hand. Her pointed chin and dark red mouth moved in an uncertain way, as if she wished to laugh again; her long black lashes flickered with the quick-moving lights in her hidden eyes.

María Concepción did not stir nor breathe for some seconds. Her forehead was cold, and yet boiling water seemed to be pouring slowly along her spine. An un-accountable pain was in her knees, as if they were broken. She was afraid Juan and María Rosa would feel her eyes fixed upon them and would find her there, un-able to move, spying upon them. But they did not pass beyond the enclosure, nor even glance towards the gap in the wall opening upon the road.

Juan lifted one of María Rosa's loosened braids and slapped her neck with it playfully. She smiled softly, consentingly. Together they moved back through the hives of honey-comb. María Rosa balanced her jar on one hip and swung her long full petticoats with every step. Juan flourished his wide hat back and forth, walking proudly as a game-cock.

María Concepción came out of the heavy cloud which enwrapped her head and bound her throat, and found herself walking onward, keeping the road without knowing it, feeling her way delicately, her ears strumming as if all María Rosa's bees had hived in them. Her careful sense of duty kept her moving toward the buried city where Juan's chief, the American archeologist, was taking his midday rest, waiting for his food.

Juan and María Rosa! She burned all over now, as if a layer of tiny fig-cactus bristles, as cruel as spun glass, had crawled under her skin. She wished to sit down quietly and wait for her death, but not until she had cut the throats of her man and that girl who were laughing and kissing under the cornstalks. Once when she was a young girl she had come back from market to find her jacal burned to a pile of ash and her few silver coins gone. A dark empty feeling had filled her; she kept moving about the place, not believing her eyes, expecting it all to take shape again before her. But it was gone, and though she knew an enemy had done it, she could not find out who it was, and could only curse and threaten the air. Now here was a worse thing, but she knew her enemy. María Rosa, that sinful girl, shameless!

8

She heard herself saying a harsh, true word about María Rosa, saying it aloud as if she expected someone to agree with her: "Yes, she is a whore! She has no right to live."

At this moment the gray untidy head of Givens appeared over the edges of the newest trench he had caused to be dug in his field of excavations. The long deep crevasses, in which a man might stand without being seen, lay crisscrossed like orderly gashes of a giant scalpel. Nearly all of the men of the community worked for Givens, helping him to uncover the lost city of their ancestors. They worked all the year through and prospered, digging every day for those small clay heads and bits of pottery and fragments of painted walls for which there was no good use on earth, being all broken and encrusted with clay. They themselves could make better ones, perfectly stout and new, which they took to town and peddled to foreigners for real money. But the unearthly delight of the chief in finding these worn-out things was an endless puzzle. He would fairly roar for joy at times, waving a shattered pot or a human skull above his head, shouting for his photographer to come and make a picture of this!

Now he emerged, and his young enthusiast's eyes welcomed María Concepción from his old-man face, covered with hard wrinkles and burned to the color of red earth. "I hope you've brought me a nice fat one." He selected a fowl from the bunch dangling nearest him as María Concepción, wordless, leaned over the trench. "Dress it for me, there's a good girl. I'll broil it."

María Concepción took the fowl by the head, and silently, swiftly drew her knife across its throat, twisting the head off with the casual firmness she might use with the top of a beet.

"Good God, woman, you do have nerve," said Givens, watching her. "I can't do that. It gives me the creeps."

"My home country is Guadalajara," explained María Concepción, without bravado, as she picked and gutted the fowl.

She stood and regarded Givens condescendingly, that diverting white man who had no woman of his own to cook for him, and moreover appeared not to feel any loss of dignity in preparing his own food. He squatted now, eyes squinted, nose wrinkled to avoid the smoke, turning the roasting fowl busily on a stick. A mysterious man, undoubtedly rich, and Juan's chief, therefore to be respected, to be placated.

"The tortillas are fresh and hot, señor," she murmured gently. "With your permission I will now go to market."

"Yes, yes, run along; bring me another of these tomorrow." Givens turned his head to look at her again. Her grand manner sometimes reminded him of royalty in exile. He noticed her unnatural paleness. "The sun is too hot, eh?" he asked.

"Yes, sir. Pardon me, but Juan will be here soon?"

"He ought to be here now. Leave his food. The others will eat it."

She moved away; the blue of her rebozo became a dancing spot in the heat waves that rose from the gray-red soil. Givens liked his Indians best when he could feel a fatherly indulgence for their primitive childish ways. He told comic stories of Juan's escapades, of how often he had saved him, in the past five years, from going to jail, and even from being shot, for his varied and always unexpected misdeeds.

"I am never a minute too soon to get him out of one pickle or another," he would say. "Well, he's a good worker, and I know how to manage him."

After Juan was married, he used to twit him, with exactly the right shade of condescension, on his many infidelities to María Concepción. "She'll catch you yet, and God help you!" he was fond of saying, and Juan would laugh with immense pleasure.

It did not occur to María Concepción to tell Juan she had found him out. During the day her anger against him died, and her anger against María Rosa grew.

She kept saying to herself, "When I was a young girl like María Rosa, if a man had caught hold of me so, I would have broken my jar over his head." She forgot completely that she had not resisted even so much as María Rosa, on the day that Juan had first taken hold of her. Besides she had married him afterwards in the church, and that was a very different thing.

Juan did not come home that night, but went away to war and María Rosa went with him. Juan had a rifle at his shoulder and two pistols at his belt. María Rosa wore a rifle also, slung on her back along with the blankets and the cooking pots. They joined the nearest detachment of troops in the field, and María Rosa marched ahead with the battalion of experienced women of war, which went over the crops like locusts, gathering provisions for the army. She cooked with them, and ate with them what was left after the men had eaten. After battles she went out on the field with the others to salvage clothing and ammunition and guns from the slain before they should begin to swell in the heat. Sometimes they would encounter the women from the other army, and a second battle as grim as the first would take place.

There was no particular scandal in the village. People shrugged, grinned. It was far better that they were gone. The neighbors went around saying that María Rosa was safer in the army than she would be in the same village with María Concepción.

María Concepción did not weep when Juan left her; and when the baby was born, and died within four days, she did not weep. "She is mere stone," said old Lupe, who went over and offered charms to preserve the baby.

"May you rot in hell with your charms," said María Concepción.

If she had not gone so regularly to church, lighting candles before the saints, kneeling with her arms spread in the form of a cross for hours at a time, and receiving holy communion every month, there might have been talk of her being devil-possessed, her face was so changed and blind-looking. But this was impossible when, after all, she had been married by the priest. It must be, they reasoned, that she was being punished for her pride. They decided that this was the true cause for everything: she was altogether too proud. So they pitied her.

During the year that Juan and María Rosa were gone María Concepción sold her fowls and looked after her garden and her sack of hard coins grew. Lupe had no talent for bees, and the hives did not prosper. She began to blame María Rosa for running away, and to praise María Concepción for her behavior. She used to see María Concepción at the market or at church, and she always said that no one could tell by looking at her now that she was a woman who had such a heavy grief.

"I pray God everything goes well with María Concepción from this out," she would say, "for she has had her share of trouble."

When some idle person repeated this to the deserted woman, she went down to Lupe's house and stood within the clearing and called to the medicine woman, who sat in her doorway stirring a mess of her infallible cure for sores: "Keep your prayers to yourself, Lupe, or offer them for others who need them. I will ask God for what I want in this world."

"And will you get it, you think, María Concepción?" asked Lupe, tittering cruelly and smelling the wooden mixing spoon. "Did you pray for what you have now?"

Afterward everyone noticed that María Concepción went oftener to church, and even seldomer to the village to talk with the other women as they sat along the curb, nursing their babies and eating fruit, at the end of the market-day.

"She is wrong to take us for enemies," said old Soledad, who was a thinker and a peace-maker. "All women have these troubles. Well, we should suffer together."

But María Concepción lived alone. She was gaunt, as if something were gnawing her away inside, her eyes were sunken, and she would not speak a word if she could help it. She worked harder than ever, and her butchering knife was scarcely ever out of her hand.

Juan and María Rosa, disgusted with military life, came home one day without asking permission of anyone. The field of war had unrolled itself, a long scroll of vexations, until the end had frayed out within twenty miles of Juan's village. So he and María Rosa, now lean as a wolf, burdened with a child daily expected, set out with no farewells to the regiment and walked home.

They arrived one morning about daybreak. Juan was picked up on sight by a group of military police from the small barracks on the edge of town, and taken to prison, where the officer in charge told him with impersonal cheerfulness that he would add one to a catch of ten waiting to be shot as deserters the next morning.

María Rosa, screaming and falling on her face in the road, was taken under the armpits by two guards and helped briskly to her jacal, now sadly run down. She was received with professional importance by Lupe, who helped the baby to be born at once.

Limping with foot soreness, a layer of dust concealing his fine new clothes got mysteriously from somewhere, Juan appeared before the captain at the barracks. The captain recognized him as head digger for his good friend Givens, and dispatched a note to Givens saying: "I am holding the person of Juan Villegas awaiting your further disposition."

When Givens showed up Juan was delivered to him with the urgent request that nothing be made public about so humane and sensible an operation on the part of military authority.

Juan walked out of the rather stifling atmosphere of the drumhead court, a definite air of swagger about him. His hat, of unreasonable dimensions and embroidered with silver thread, hung over one eyebrow, secured at the back by a cord of silver dripping with bright blue tassels. His shirt was of a checkerboard pattern in green and black, his white cotton trousers were bound by a belt of yellow leather tooled in red. His feet were bare, full of stone bruises, and sadly ragged as to toenails. He removed his cigarette from the corner of his full-lipped wide mouth. He removed the splendid hat. His black dusty hair, pressed moistly to his forehead, sprang up suddenly in a cloudy thatch on his crown. He bowed to the officer, who appeared to be gazing at a vacuum. He swung his arm wide in a free circle upsoaring towards the prison window, where forlorn heads poked over the window sill, hot eyes following after the lucky departing one. Two or three of the heads nodded, and a half dozen hands were flipped at him in an effort to imitate his own casual and heady manner.

Juan kept up this insufferable pantomime until they rounded the first clump of fig-cactus. Then he seized Givens' hand and burst into oratory. "Blessed be the day your servant Juan Villegas first came under your eyes. From this day my life is yours without condition, ten thousand thanks with all my heart!"

"For God's sake stop playing the fool," said Givens irritably. "Some day I'm going to be five minutes too late."

"Well, it is nothing much to be shot, my chief—certainly you know I was not afraid—but to be shot in a drove of deserters, against a cold wall, just in the moment of my home-coming, by order of that . . ."

Glittering epithets tumbled over one another like explosions of a rocket. All the scandalous analogies from the animal and vegetable worlds were applied in a vivid, unique and personal way to the life, loves, and family history of the officer who had just set him free. When he had quite cursed himself dry, and his nerves were soothed, he added: "With your permission, my chief!"

"What will María Concepción say to all this?" asked Givens. "You are very informal, Juan, for a man who was married in the church."

Juan put on his hat.

"Oh, María Concepción! That's nothing. Look, my chief, to be married in the church is a great misfortune for a man. After that he is not himself any more. How can that woman complain when I do not drink even at fiestas enough to be really drunk? I do not beat her; never, never. We were always at peace. I say to her, Come here, and she comes straight. I say, Go there, and she goes quickly. Yet sometimes I looked at her and thought, Now I am married to that woman in the church, and I felt a sinking inside, as if something were lying heavy on my stomach. With María Rosa it is all different. She is not silent; she talks. When she talks too much, I slap her and say, Silence, thou simpleton! and she weeps. She is just a girl with whom I do as I please. You know how she used to keep those clean little bees in their hives? She is like their honey to me. I swear it. I would not harm María Concepción because I am married to her in the church; but also, my chief, I will not leave María Rosa, because she pleases me more than any other woman."

"Let me tell you, Juan, things haven't been going as well as you think. You be careful. Some day María Concepción will just take your head off with that carving knife of hers. You keep that in mind."

Juan's expression was the proper blend of masculine triumph and sentimental melancholy. It was pleasant to

18

see himself in the rôle of hero to two such desirable women. He had just escaped from the threat of a disagreeable end. His clothes were new and handsome, and they had cost him just nothing. María Rosa had collected them for him here and there after battles. He was walking in the early sunshine, smelling the good smells of ripening cactus-figs, peaches, and melons, of pungent berries dangling from the pepper-trees, and the smoke of his cigarette under his nose. He was on his way to civilian life with his patient chief. His situation was ineffably perfect, and he swallowed it whole.

"My chief," he addressed Givens handsomely, as one man of the world to another, "women are good things, but not at this moment. With your permission, I will now go to the village and eat. My God, *how* I shall eat! Tomorrow morning very early I will come to the buried city and work like seven men. Let us forget María Concepción and María Rosa. Each one in her place. I will manage them when the time comes."

News of Juan's adventure soon got abroad, and Juan found many friends about him during the morning. They frankly commended his way of leaving the army. It was in itself the act of a hero. The new hero ate a great deal and drank somewhat, the occasion being better than a feast-day. It was almost noon before he returned to visit María Rosa.

He found her sitting on a clean straw mat, rubbing fat on her three-hour-old son. Before this felicitous vision Juan's emotions so twisted him that he returned to the village and invited every man in the "Death and Resurrection" pulque shop to drink with him.

Having thus taken leave of his balance, he started back to María Rosa, and found himself unaccountably in his own house, attempting to beat María Concepción by way of reëstablishing himself in his legal household.

María Concepción, knowing all the events of that unhappy day, was not in a yielding mood, and refused to be beaten. She did not scream nor implore; she stood her ground and resisted; she even struck at him. Juan, amazed, hardly knowing what he did, stepped back and gazed at her inquiringly through a leisurely whirling film which seemed to have lodged behind his eyes. Certainly he had not even thought of touching her. Oh, well, no harm done. He gave up, turned away, half-asleep on his feet. He dropped amiably in a shadowed corner and began to snore.

María Concepción, seeing that he was quiet, began to bind the legs of her fowls. It was market-day and she was late. She fumbled and tangled the bits of cord in her haste, and set off across the plowed fields instead of taking the accustomed road. She ran with a crazy panic in her head, her stumbling legs. Now and then she would stop and look about her, trying to place her-self, then go on a few steps, until she realized that she was not going towards the market.

At once she came to her senses completely, recognized the thing that troubled her so terribly, was certain of what she wanted. She sat down quietly under a shelter-ing thorny bush and gave herself over to her long devouring sorrow. The thing which had for so long squeezed her whole body into a tight dumb knot of suffering suddenly broke with shocking violence. She jerked with the involuntary recoil of one who receives a blow, and the sweat poured from her skin as if the wounds of her whole life were shedding their salt ichor. Drawing her rebozo over her head, she bowed her fore-head on her updrawn knees, and sat there in deadly silence and immobility. From time to time she lifted her head where the sweat formed steadily and poured down her face, drenching the front of her chemise, and her mouth had the shape of crying, but there were no tears and no sound. All her being was a dark confused mem-ory of grief burning in her at night, of deadly baffled anger eating at her by day, until her very tongue tasted bitter, and her feet were as heavy as if she were mired in the muddy roads during the time of rains.

21

After a great while she stood up and threw the rebozo off her face, and set out walking again.

Juan awakened slowly, with long yawns and grumblings, alternated with short relapses into sleep full of visions and clamors. A blur of orange light seared his eyeballs when he tried to unseal his lids. There came from somewhere a low voice weeping without tears, saying meaningless phrases over and over. He began to listen. He tugged at the leash of his stupor, he strained to grasp those words which terrified him even though he could not quite hear them. Then he came awake with frightening suddenness, sitting up and staring at the long sharpened streak of light piercing the corn-husk walls from the level disappearing sun.

María Concepción stood in the doorway, looming colossally tall to his betrayed eyes. She was talking quickly, and calling his name. Then he saw her clearly.

"God's name!" said Juan, frozen to the marrow, "here I am facing my death!" for the long knife she wore habitually at her belt was in her hand. But instead, she threw it away, clear from her, and got down on her knees, crawling toward him as he had seen her crawl many times toward the shrine at Guadalupe Villa. He watched her approach with such horror that the hair of his head seemed to be lifting itself away from him. Falling forward upon her face, she huddled over him, lips moving in a ghostly whisper. Her words became clear, and Juan understood them all.

For a second he could not move nor speak. Then he took her head between both his hands, and supported her in this way, saying swiftly, anxiously reassuring, almost in a babble:

"Oh, thou poor creature! Oh, madwoman! Oh, my María Concepción, unfortunate! Listen. . . . Don't be afraid. Listen to me! I will hide thee away, I thy own man will protect thee! Quiet! Not a sound!"

Trying to collect himself, he held her and cursed under his breath for a few moments in the gathering darkness. María Concepción bent over, face almost on the ground, her feet folded under her, as if she would hide behind him. For the first time in his life Juan was aware of danger. This was danger. María Concepción would be dragged away between two gendarmes, with him following helpless and unarmed, to spend the rest of her days in Belén Prison, maybe. Danger! The night swarmed with threats. He stood up and dragged her up with him. She was silent and perfectly rigid, holding to him with resistless strength, her hands stiffened on his arms.

"Get me the knife," he told her in a whisper. She

obeyed, her feet slipping along the hard earth floor, her shoulders straight, her arms close to her side. He lighted a candle. María Concepción held the knife out to him. It was stained and dark even to the handle with drying blood.

He frowned at her harshly, noting the same stains on her chemise and hands.

"Take off thy clothes and wash thy hands," he ordered. He washed the knife carefully, and threw the water wide of the doorway. She watched him and did likewise with the bowl in which she had bathed.

"Light the brasero and cook food for me," he told her in the same peremptory tone. He took her garments and went out. When he returned, she was wearing an old soiled dress, and was fanning the fire in the charcoal burner. Seating himself cross-legged near her, he stared at her as at a creature unknown to him, who bewildered him utterly, for whom there was no possible explanation. She did not turn her head, but kept silent and still, except for the movements of her strong hands fanning the blaze which cast sparks and small jets of white smoke, flaring and dying rhythmically with the motion of the fan, lighting her face and darkening it by turns.

Juan's voice barely disturbed the silence: "Listen to me carefully, and tell me the truth, and when the gendarmes come here for us, thou shalt have nothing to fear. But there will be something for us to settle between us afterward."

The light from the charcoal burner shone in her eyes; a yellow phosphorescence glimmered behind the dark iris.

"For me everything is settled now," she answered, in a tone so tender, so grave, so heavy with suffering, that Juan felt his vitals contract. He wished to repent openly, not as a man, but as a very small child. He could not fathom her, nor himself, nor the mysterious fortunes of life grown so instantly confused where all had seemed so gay and simple. He felt too that she had become invaluable, a woman without equal among a million women, and he could not tell why. He drew an enormous sigh that rattled in his chest.

"Yes, yes, it is all settled. I shall not go away again. We must stay here together."

Whispering, he questioned her and she answered whispering, and he instructed her over and over until she had her lesson by heart. The hostile darkness of the night encroached upon them, flowing over the narrow threshold, invading their hearts. It brought with it sighs and murmurs, the pad of secretive feet in the near-by road, the sharp staccato whimper of wind through the cactus leaves. All these familiar, once friendly cadences were now invested with sinister terrors; a dread, formless and uncontrollable, took hold of them both.

"Light another candle," said Juan, loudly, in too resolute, too sharp a tone. "Let us eat now."

They sat facing each other and ate from the same dish, after their old habit. Neither tasted what they ate. With food half-way to his mouth, Juan listened. The sound of voices rose, spread, widened at the turn of the road along the cactus wall. A spray of lantern light shot through the hedge, a single voice slashed the blackness, ripped the fragile layer of silence suspended above the hut.

"Juan Villegas!"

"Pass, friends!" Juan roared back cheerfully.

They stood in the doorway, simple cautious gendarmes from the village, mixed-bloods themselves with Indian sympathies, well known to all the community. They flashed their lanterns almost apologetically upon the pleasant, harmless scene of a man eating supper with his wife.

"Pardon, brother," said the leader. "Someone has killed the woman María Rosa, and we must question her neighbors and friends." He paused, and added with an attempt at severity, "Naturally!"

"Naturally," agreed Juan. "You know that I was a good friend of María Rosa. This is bad news."

26

They all went away together, the men walkin,
group, María Concepción following a few steps i
rear, near Juan. No one spoke.

The two points of candlelight at María Rosa's head flu
tered uneasily; the shadows shifted and dodged on th
stained darkened walls. To María Concepción everything
in the smothering enclosing room shared an evil restless-
ness. The watchful faces of those called as witnesses,
the faces of old friends, were made alien by the look of
speculation in their eyes. The ridges of the rose-colored
rebozo thrown over the body varied continually, as
though the thing it covered was not perfectly in repose.
Her eyes swerved over the body in the open painted
coffin, from the candle tips at the head to the feet, jut-
ting up thinly, the small scarred soles protruding, freshly
washed, a mass of crooked, half-healed wounds, thorn-
pricks and cuts of sharp stones. Her gaze went back to
the candle flame, to Juan's eyes warning her, to the gendarmes talking among themselves. Her eyes would not
be controlled.

With a leap that shook her her gaze settled upon the
face of María Rosa. Instantly her blood ran smoothly
again: there was nothing to fear. Even the restless light
could not give a look of life to that fixed countenance.

27

She was dead. María Concepción felt her muscles give way softly; her heart began beating steadily without effort. She knew no more rancor against that pitiable thing, lying indifferently in its blue coffin under the fine silk rebozo. The mouth drooped sharply at the corners in a grimace of weeping arrested half-way. The brows were distressed; the dead flesh could not cast off the shape of its last terror. It was all finished. María Rosa had eaten too much honey and had had too much love. Now she must sit in hell, crying over her sins and her hard death forever and ever.

Old Lupe's cackling voice arose. She had spent the morning helping María Rosa, and it had been hard work. The child had spat blood the moment it was born, a bad sign. She thought then that bad luck would come to the house. Well, about sunset she was in the yard at the back of the house grinding tomatoes and peppers. She had left mother and babe asleep. She heard a strange noise in the house, a choking and smothered calling, like someone wailing in sleep. Well, such a thing is only natural. But there followed a light, quick, thudding sound—

"Like the blows of a fist?" interrupted an officer.

"No, not at all like such a thing."

"How do you know?"

"I am well acquainted with that sound, friends," retorted Lupe. "This was something else."

She was at a loss to describe it exactly. A moment later, there came the sound of pebbles rolling and slipping under feet; then she knew someone had been there and was running away.

"Why did you wait so long before going to see?"

"I am old and hard in the joints," said Lupe. "I cannot run after people. I walked as fast as I could to the cactus hedge, for it is only by this way that anyone can enter. There was no one in the road, sir, no one. Three cows, with a dog driving them; nothing else. When I got to María Rosa, she was lying all tangled up, and from her neck to her middle she was full of knife-holes. It was a sight to move the Blessed Image Himself! Her eyes were—"

"Never mind. Who came oftenest to her house before she went away? Did you know her enemies?"

Lupe's face congealed, closed. Her spongy skin drew into a network of secretive wrinkles. She turned withdrawn and expressionless eyes upon the gendarmes.

"I am an old woman. I do not see well. I cannot hurry on my feet. I know no enemy of María Rosa. I did not see anyone leave the clearing."

"You did not hear splashing in the spring near the bridge?"

"No, sir."

"Why, then, do our dogs follow a scent there and lose it?"

"God only knows, my friend. I am an old wo—"

"Yes. How did the footfalls sound?"

"Like the tread of an evil spirit!" Lupe broke forth in a swelling oracular tone that startled them. The Indians stirred uneasily, glanced at the dead, then at Lupe. They half expected her to produce the evil spirit among them at once.

The gendarme began to lose his temper.

"No, poor unfortunate; I mean, were they heavy or light? The footsteps of a man or of a woman? Was the person shod or barefoot?"

A glance at the listening circle assured Lupe of their thrilled attention. She enjoyed the dangerous importance of her situation. She could have ruined that María Concepción with a word, but it was even sweeter to make fools of these gendarmes who went about spying on honest people. She raised her voice again. What she had not seen she could not describe, thank God! No one could harm her because her knees were stiff and she could not run even to seize a murderer. As for knowing the difference between footfalls, shod or bare, man or woman, nay, between devil and human, who ever heard of such madness?

"My eyes are not ears, gentlemen," she ended grandly, "but upon my heart I swear those footsteps fell as the tread of the spirit of evil!"

"Imbecile!" yapped the leader in a shrill voice. "Take her away, one of you! Now, Juan Villegas, tell me—"

Juan told his story patiently, several times over. He had returned to his wife that day. She had gone to market as usual. He had helped her prepare her fowls. She had returned about mid-afternoon, they had talked, she had cooked, they had eaten, nothing was amiss. Then the gendarmes came with the news about María Rosa. That was all. Yes, María Rosa had run away with him, but there had been no bad blood between him and his wife on this account, nor between his wife and María Rosa. Everybody knew that his wife was a quiet woman.

María Concepción heard her own voice answering without a break. It was true at first she was troubled when her husband went away, but after that she had not worried about him. It was the way of men, she believed. She was a church-married woman and knew her place. Well, he had come home at last. She had gone to market, but had come back early, because now she had her man to cook for. That was all.

Other voices broke in. A toothless old man said: "She is a woman of good reputation among us, and María Rosa was not." A smiling young mother, Anita, baby at breast, said: "If no one thinks so, how can you accuse her? It was the loss of her child and not of her husband that changed her so." Another: "María Rosa had a strange life, apart from us. How do we know who might have come from another place to do her evil?" And old Soledad spoke up boldly: "When I saw María Concepción in the market today, I said, 'Good luck to you, María Concepción, this is a happy day for you!' " and she gave María Concepción a long easy stare, and the smile of a born wise-woman.

María Concepción suddenly felt herself guarded, surrounded, upborne by her faithful friends. They were around her, speaking for her, defending her, the forces of life were ranged invincibly with her against the beaten dead. María Rosa had thrown away her share of strength in them, she lay forfeited among them. María Concepción looked from one to the other of the circling, intent faces. Their eyes gave back reassurance, understanding, a secret and mighty sympathy.

The gendarmes were at a loss. They, too, felt that sheltering wall cast impenetrably around her. They were certain she had done it, and yet they could not accuse her. Nobody could be accused; there was not a shred of true evidence. They shrugged their shoulders and snapped their fingers and shuffled their feet. Well, then, good night to everybody. Many pardons for having intruded. Good health!

A small bundle lying against the wall at the head of the coffin squirmed like an eel. A wail, a mere sliver of sound, issued. María Concepción took the son of María Rosa in her arms.

"He is mine," she said clearly, "I will take him with me."

No one assented in words, but an approving nod, a bare breath of complete agreement, stirred among them as they made way for her.

María Concepción, carrying the child, followed Juan from the clearing. The hut was left with its lighted candles and a crowd of old women who would sit up all night, drinking coffee and smoking and telling ghost stories.

Juan's exaltation had burned out. There was not an ember of excitement left in him. He was tired. The perilous adventure was over. María Rosa had vanished, to come no more forever. Their days of marching, of eating, of quarreling and making love between battles, were all over. Tomorrow he would go back to dull and endless labor, he must descend into the trenches of the buried city as María Rosa must go into her grave. He

33

felt his veins fill up with bitterness, with black unendurable melancholy. Oh, Jesus! what bad luck overtakes a man!

Well, there was no way out of it now. For the moment he craved only to sleep. He was so drowsy he could scarcely guide his feet. The occasional light touch of the woman at his elbow was as unreal, as ghostly as the brushing of a leaf against his face. He did not know why he had fought to save her, and now he forgot her. There was nothing in him except a vast blind hurt like a covered wound.

He entered the jacal, and without waiting to light a candle, threw off his clothing, sitting just within the door. He moved with lagging, half-awake hands, to strip his body of its heavy finery. With a long groaning sigh of relief he fell straight back on the floor, almost instantly asleep, his arms flung up and outward.

María Concepción, a small clay jar in her hand, approached the gentle little mother goat tethered to a sapling, which gave and yielded as she pulled at the rope's end after the farthest reaches of grass about her. The kid, tied up a few feet away, rose bleating, its feathery fleece shivering in the fresh wind. Sitting on her heels, holding his tether, she allowed him to suckle a few moments. Afterward—all her movements very deliberate and even—she drew a supply of milk for the child.

She sat against the wall ot her house, near the doorway. The child, fed and asleep, was cradled in the hollow of her crossed legs. The silence overfilled the world, the skies flowed down evenly to the rim of the valley, the stealthy moon crept slantwise to the shelter of the mountains. She felt soft and warm all over; she dreamed that the newly born child was her own, and she was resting deliciously.

María Concepción could hear Juan's breathing. The sound vapored from the low doorway, calmly; the house seemed to be resting after a burdensome day. She breathed, too, very slowly and quietly, each inspiration saturating her with repose. The child's light, faint breath was a mere shadowy moth of sound in the silver air. The night, the earth under her, seemed to swell and recede together with a limitless, unhurried, benign breathing. She drooped and closed her eyes, feeling the slow rise and fall within her own body. She did not know what it was, but it eased her all through. Even as she was falling asleep, head bowed over the child, she was still aware of a strange, wakeful happiness.

MAGIC

MAGIC

Magic

AND, Madame Blanchard, believe that I am happy to
be here with you and your family because it is so serene,
everything, and before this I worked for a long time in
a fancy house—maybe you don't know what is a fancy
house? Naturally . . . everyone must have heard sometime or other. Well, Madame, I work always where there
is work to be had, and so in this place I worked very
hard all hours, and saw too many things, things you
wouldn't believe, and I wouldn't think of telling you,
only maybe it will rest you while I brush your hair.
You'll excuse me too but I could not help hearing you
say to the laundress maybe someone had bewitched
your linens, they fall away so fast in the wash. Well,
there was a girl there in that house, a poor thing, thin,
but well-liked by all the men who called, and you understand she could not get along with the woman who ran
the house. They quarreled, the madam cheated her on
her checks: you know, the girl got a check, a brass one,
every time, and at the week's end she gave those back
to the madam, yes, that was the way, and got her per-
centage, a very small little of her earnings: it is a business,

you see, like any other—and the madam used to pretend
the girl had given back only so many checks, you see,
and really she had given many more, but after they were
out of her hands, what could she do? So she would say,
I will get out of this place, and curse and cry. Then the
madam would hit her over the head. She always hit
people over the head with bottles, it was the way she
fought. My good heavens, Madame Blanchard, what confusion there would be sometimes with a girl running
raving downstairs, and the madam pulling her back by
the hair and smashing a bottle on her forehead.

It was nearly always about the money, the girls got
in debt so, and if they wished to go they could not without paying every sou marqué. The madam had full
understanding with the police; the girls must come back
with them or go to the jails. Well, they always came
back with the policemen or with another kind of man
friend of the madam: she could make men work for
her too, but she paid them very well for all, let me tell
you: and so the girls stayed on unless they were sick;
if so, if they got too sick, she sent them away again.

Madame Blanchard said, "You are pulling a little here,"
and eased a strand of hair: "and then what?"

Pardon—but this girl, there was a true hatred between
her and the madam. She would say many times, I make
more money than anybody else in the house, and every

week were scenes. So at last she said one morning, Now I will leave this place, and she took out forty dollars from under her pillow and said, Here's your money! The madam began to shout, Where did you get all that, you ——? and accused her of robbing the men who came to visit her. The girl said, Keep your hands off or I'll brain you: and at that the madam took hold of her shoulders, and began to lift her knee and kick this girl most terribly in the stomach, and even in her most secret place, Madame Blanchard, and then she beat her in the face with a bottle, and the girl fell back again into her room where I was making clean. I helped her to the bed, and she sat there holding her sides with her head hanging down, and when she got up again there was blood everywhere she had sat. So then the madam came in once more and screamed, Now you can get out, you are no good for me any more: I don't repeat all, you understand it is too much. But she took all the money she could find, and at the door she gave the girl a great push in the back with her knee, so that she fell again in the street, and then got up and went away with the dress barely on her.

After this the men who knew this girl kept saying, Where is Ninette? And they kept asking this in the next days, so that the madam could not say any longer, I put her out because she is a thief. No, she began to see she was wrong to send this Ninette away, and then she said, She will be back in a few days, don't trouble yourself.

And now, Madame Blanchard, if you wish to hear, I come to the strange part, the thing recalled to me when you said your linens were bewitched. For the cook in that place was a woman, colored like myself, like myself with much French blood just the same, like myself living always among people who worked spells. But she had a very hard heart, she helped the madam in everything, she liked to watch all that happened, and she gave away tales on the girls. The madam trusted her above everything, and she said, Well, where can I find that slut? because she had gone altogether out of Basin Street before the madam began to ask the police to bring her again. Well, the cook said, I know a charm that works here in New Orleans, colored women do it to bring back their men: in seven days they come again very happy to stay and they cannot say why: even your enemy will come back to you believing you are his friend. It is a New Orleans charm for sure, for certain, they say it does not work even across the river. . . . And then they did it just as the cook said. They took the chamber pot of this girl from under her bed, and in it they mixed with water and milk all the relics of her they found there: the hair from her brush, and the face powder from the puff, and even little bits of her nails they found about the edges of the carpet where she sat by habit to cut her finger- and toe-nails; and they dipped the sheets with her blood into the water, and all the time the cook said something over it in a low voice; I could not hear all, but at last she said to the madam, Now spit in it: and the madam spat, and the cook said, When she comes back she will be dirt under your feet.

Madame Blanchard closed her perfume bottle with a thin click: "Yes, and then?"

Then in seven nights the girl came back and she looked very sick, the same clothes and all, but happy to be there. One of the men said, Welcome home, Ninette! and when she started to speak to the madam, the madam said, Shut up and get upstairs and dress yourself. So Ninette, this girl, she said, I'll be down in just a minute. And after that she lived there quietly.

ROPE

Rope

ON the third day after they moved to the country he
came walking back from the village carrying a basket
of groceries and a twenty-four-yard coil of rope. She
came out to meet him, wiping her hands on her green
smock. Her hair was tumbled, her nose was scarlet with
sunburn; he told her that already she looked like a born
country woman. His gray flannel shirt stuck to him, his
heavy shoes were dusty. She assured him he looked like
a rural character in a play.

Had he brought the coffee? She had been waiting all
day long for coffee. They had forgot it when they ordered at the store the first day.

Gosh, no, he hadn't. Lord, now he'd have to go back.
Yes, he would if it killed him. He thought, though, he
had everything else. She reminded him it was only because he didn't drink coffee himself. If he did he would
remember it quick enough. Suppose they ran out of
cigarettes? Then she saw the rope. What was that for?
Well, he thought it might do to hang clothes on, or
something. Naturally she asked him if he thought they
were going to run a laundry? They already had a fifty-

foot line hanging right before his eyes? Why, hadn't
he noticed it, really? It was a blot on the landscape to
her.

He thought there were a lot of things a rope might
come in handy for. She wanted to know what, for in-
stance. He thought a few seconds, but nothing occurred.
They could wait and see, couldn't they? You need all
sorts of strange odds and ends around a place in the
country. She said, yes, that was so; but she thought just
at that time when every penny counted, it seemed funny
to buy more rope. That was all. She hadn't meant anything else. She hadn't just seen, not at first, why he felt
it was necessary.

Well, thunder, he had bought it because he wanted to,
and that was all there was to it. She thought that was
reason enough, and couldn't understand why he hadn't
said so, at first. Undoubtedly it would be useful, twenty-
four yards of rope, there were hundreds of things, she
couldn't think of any at the moment, but it would come
in. Of course. As he had said, things always did in the
country.

But she was a little disappointed about the coffee, and
oh, look, look, look at the eggs! Oh, my, they're all
running! What had he put on top of them? Hadn't he
known eggs mustn't be squeezed? Squeezed, who had
squeezed them, he wanted to know. What a silly thing

to say. He had simply brought them along in the basket with the other things. If they got broke it was the grocer's fault. He should know better than to put heavy things on top of eggs.

She believed it was the rope. That was the heaviest thing in the pack, she saw him plainly when he came in from the road, the rope was a big package on top of everything. He desired the whole wide world to witness that this was not a fact. He had carried the rope in one hand and the basket in the other, and what was the use of her having eyes if that was the best they could do for her?

Well, anyhow, she could see one thing plain: no eggs for breakfast. They'd have to scramble them now, for supper. It was too damned bad. She had planned to have steak for supper. No ice, meat wouldn't keep. He wanted to know why she couldn't finish breaking the eggs in a bowl and set them in a cool place.

Cool place! if he could find one for her, she'd be glad to set them there. Well, then, it seemed to him they might very well cook the meat at the same time they cooked the eggs and then warm up the meat for tomorrow. The idea simply choked her. Warmed-over meat, when they might as well have had it fresh. Second best and scraps and makeshifts, even to the meat! He rubbed her shoulder a little. It doesn't really matter so

49

much, does it, darling? Sometimes when they were play-
ful, he would rub her shoulder and she would arch and
purr. This time she hissed and almost clawed. He was
getting ready to say that they could surely manage somehow when she turned on him and said, if he told her
they could manage somehow she would certainly slap
his face.

He swallowed the words red hot, his face burned.
He picked up the rope and started to put it on the top
shelf. She would not have it on the top shelf, the jars
and tins belonged there; positively she would not have
the top shelf cluttered up with a lot of rope. She had
borne all the clutter she meant to bear in the flat in
town, there was space here at least and she meant to
keep things in order.

Well, in that case, he wanted to know what the hammer and nails were doing up there? And why had she
put them there when she knew very well he needed that
hammer and those nails upstairs to fix the window sashes?
She simply slowed down everything and made double
work on the place with her insane habit of changing
things around and hiding them.

She was sure she begged his pardon, and if she had
had any reason to believe he was going to fix the sashes
this summer she would have left the hammer and nails
right where he put them; in the middle of the bedroom

floor where they could step on them in the dark. And now if he didn't clear the whole mess out of there she would throw them down the well.

Oh, all right, all right—could he put them in the closet? Naturally not, there were brooms and mops and dustpans in the closet, and why couldn't he find a place for his rope outside her kitchen? Had he stopped to consider there were seven God-forsaken rooms in the house, and only one kitchen?

He wanted to know what of it? And did she realize she was making a complete fool of herself? And what did she take him for, a three-year-old idiot? The whole trouble with her was she needed something weaker than she was to heckle and tyrannize over. He wished to God now they had a couple of children she could take it out on. Maybe he'd get some rest.

Her face changed at this, she reminded him he had forgot the coffee and had bought a worthless piece of rope. And when she thought of all the things they actually needed to make the place even decently fit to live in, well, she could cry, that was all. She looked so forlorn, so lost and despairing he couldn't believe it was only a piece of rope that was causing all the racket. What *was* the matter, for God's sake?

Oh, would he please hush and go away, and *stay* away, if he could, for five minutes? By all means, yes, he would. He'd stay away indefinitely if she wished. Lord, yes, there was nothing he'd like better than to clear out and never come back. She couldn't for the life of her see what was holding him, then. It was a swell time. Here she was, stuck, miles from a railroad, with a half-empty house on her hands, and not a penny in her pocket, and everything on earth to do; it seemed the God-sent moment for him to get out from under. She was surprised he hadn't stayed in town as it was until she had come out and done the work and got things straightened out. It was his usual trick.

It appeared to him that this was going a little far. Just a touch out of bounds, if she didn't mind his saying so. Why the hell had he stayed in town the summer before? To do a half-dozen extra jobs to get the money he had sent her. That was it. She knew perfectly well they couldn't have done it otherwise. She had agreed with him at the time. And that was the only time so help him he had ever left her to do anything by herself.

Oh, he could tell that to his great-grandmother. She had her notion of what had kept him in town. Considerably more than a notion, if he wanted to know. So, she was going to bring all that up again, was she? Well, she could just think what she pleased. He was tired of explaining. It may have looked funny but he had simply got hooked in, and what could he do? It was impossible to believe that she was going to take it seriously. Yes, yes, she knew how it was with a man: if he was left by himself a minute, some woman was certain to kidnap him. And naturally he couldn't hurt her feelings by refusing!

Well, what was she raving about? Did she forget she had told him those two weeks alone in the country were the happiest she had known for four years? And how long had they been married when she said that? All right, shut up! If she thought that hadn't stuck in his craw.

She hadn't meant she was happy because she was away from him. She meant she was happy getting the devilish house nice and ready for him. That was what she had meant, and now look! Bringing up something she had said a year ago simply to justify himself for forgetting her coffee and breaking the eggs and buying a wretched piece of rope they couldn't afford. She really thought it was time to drop the subject, and now she wanted only two things in the world. She wanted him to get that rope from underfoot, and go back to the village and get her coffee, and if he could remember it, he might bring a metal mitt for the skillets, and two more curtain rods, and if there were any rubber gloves in the village, her hands were simply raw, and a bottle of milk of magnesia from the drugstore.

Rope

He looked out at the dark blue afternoon sweltering on the slopes, and mopped his forehead and sighed heavily and said, if only she could wait a minute for *anything*, he was going back. He had said so, hadn't he, the very instant they found he had overlooked it?

Oh, yes, well . . . run along. She was going to wash windows. The country was so beautiful! She doubted they'd have a moment to enjoy it. He meant to go, but he could not until he had said that if she wasn't such a hopeless melancholiac she might see that this was only for a few days. Couldn't she remember anything pleasant about the other summers? Hadn't they ever had any fun? She hadn't time to talk about it, and now would he please not leave that rope lying around for her to trip on? He picked it up, somehow it had toppled off the table, and walked out with it under his arm.

Was he going this minute? He certainly was. She thought so. Sometimes it seemed to her he had second sight about the precisely perfect moment to leave her ditched. She had meant to put the mattresses out to sun, if they put them out this minute they would get at least three hours, he must have heard her say that morning she meant to put them out. So of course he would walk off and leave her to it. She supposed he thought the exercise would do her good.

Well, he was merely going to get her coffee. A four-mile walk for two pounds of coffee was ridiculous, but he was perfectly willing to do it. The habit was making a wreck of her, but if she wanted to wreck herself there was nothing he could do about it. If he thought it was coffee that was making a wreck of her, she congratulated him: he must have a damned easy conscience.

Conscience or no conscience, he didn't see why the mattresses couldn't very well wait until tomorrow. And anyhow, for God's sake, were they living *in* the house, or were they going to let the house ride them to death? She paled at this, her face grew livid about the mouth, she looked quite dangerous, and reminded him that housekeeping was no more her work than it was his: she had other work to do as well, and when did he think she was going to find time to do it at this rate?

Was she going to start on that again? She knew as well as he did that his work brought in the regular money, hers was only occasional, if they depended on what *she* made—and she might as well get straight on this question once for all!

That was positively not the point. The question was, when both of them were working on their own time, was there going to be a division of the housework, or wasn't there? She merely wanted to know, she had to make her plans. Why, he thought that was all arranged.

It was understood that he was to help. Hadn't he always, in summers?

Hadn't he, though? Oh, just hadn't he? And when, and where, and doing what? Lord, what an uproarious joke!

It was such a very uproarious joke that her face turned slightly purple, and she screamed with laughter. She laughed so hard she had to sit down, and finally a rush of tears spurted from her eyes and poured down into the lifted corners of her mouth. He dashed towards her and dragged her up to her feet and tried to pour water on her head. The dipper hung by a string on a nail and he broke it loose. Then he tried to pump water with one hand while she struggled in the other. So he gave it up and shook her instead.

She wrenched away, crying out for him to take his rope and go to hell, she had simply given him up: and ran. He heard her high-heeled bedroom slippers clattering and stumbling on the stairs.

He went out around the house and into the lane; he suddenly realized he had a blister on his heel and his shirt felt as if it were on fire. Things broke so suddenly you didn't know where you were. She could work herself into a fury about simply nothing. She was terrible, damn it: not an ounce of reason. You might as well talk to a sieve as that woman when she got going. Damned if

he'd spend his life humoring her! Well, what to do now?
He would take back the rope and exchange it for something else. Things accumulated, things were mountain-
ous, you couldn't move them or sort them out or get rid
of them. They just lay and rotted around. He'd take it
back. Hell, why should he? He wanted it. What was
it anyhow? A piece of rope. Imagine anybody caring
more about a piece of rope than about a man's feelings.
What earthly right had she to say a word about it?
He remembered all the useless, meaningless things she
bought for herself: Why? because I wanted it, that's
why! He stopped and selected a large stone by the road.
He would put the rope behind it. He would put it in
the tool-box when he got back. He'd heard enough
about it to last him a life-time.

When he came back she was leaning against the post
box beside the road waiting. It was pretty late, the smell
of broiled steak floated nose high in the cooling air. Her
face was young and smooth and fresh-looking. Her
unmanageable funny black hair was all on end. She
waved to him from a distance, and he speeded up. She
called out that supper was ready and waiting, was he
starved?

You bet he was starved. Here was the coffee. He
waved it at her. She looked at his other hand. What was
that he had there?

Well, it was the rope again. He stopped short. He had meant to exchange it but forgot. She wanted to know why he should exchange it, if it was something he really wanted. Wasn't the air sweet now, and wasn't it fine to be here?

She walked beside him with one hand hooked into his leather belt. She pulled and jostled him a little as he walked, and leaned against him. He put his arm clear around her and patted her stomach. They exchanged wary smiles. Coffee, coffee for the Ootsum-Wootsums! He felt as if he were bringing her a beautiful present.

He was a love, she firmly believed, and if she had had her coffee in the morning, she wouldn't have behaved so funny . . . There was a whippoorwill still coming back, imagine, clear out of season, sitting in the crab-apple tree calling all by himself. Maybe his girl stood him up. Maybe she did. She hoped to hear him once more, she loved whippoorwills . . . He knew how she was, didn't he?

Sure, he knew how she was.

HE

He

LIFE was very hard for the Whipples. It was hard to feed all the hungry mouths, it was hard to keep the children in flannels during the winter, short as it was: "God knows what would become of us if we lived north," they would say: keeping them decently clean was hard. "It looks like our luck won't never let up on us," said Mr. Whipple, but Mrs. Whipple was all for taking what was sent and calling it good, anyhow when the neighbors were in earshot. "Don't ever let a soul hear us complain," she kept saying to her husband. She couldn't stand to be pitied. "No, not if it comes to it that we have to live in a wagon and pick cotton around the country," she said, "nobody's going to get a chance to look down on us."

Mrs. Whipple loved her second son, the simple-minded one, better than she loved the other two children put together. She was forever saying so, and when she talked with certain of her neighbors, she would even throw in her husband and her mother for good measure.

"You needn't keep on saying it around," said Mr. Whipple, "you'll make people think nobody else has any feelings about Him but you."

He

"It's natural for a mother," Mrs. Whipple would remind him. "You know yourself it's more natural for a mother to be that way. People don't expect so much of fathers, some way."

This didn't keep the neighbors from talking plainly among themselves. "A Lord's pure mercy if He should die," they said. "It's the sins of the fathers," they agreed among themselves. "There's bad blood and bad doings somewhere, you can bet on that." This behind the Whipples' backs. To their faces everybody said, "He's not so bad off. He'll be all right yet. Look how He grows!"

Mrs. Whipple hated to talk about it, she tried to keep her mind off it, but every time anybody set foot in the house, the subject always came up, and she had to talk about Him first, before she could get on to anything else. It seemed to ease her mind. "I wouldn't have anything happen to Him for all the world, but it just looks like I can't keep Him out of mischief. He's so strong and active, He's always into everything; He was like that since He could walk. It's actually funny sometimes, the way He can do anything; it's laughable to see Him up to His tricks. Emly has more accidents; I'm forever tying up her bruises, and Adna can't fall a foot without cracking a bone. But He can do anything and not get a scratch. The preacher said such a nice

62

thing once when he was here. He said, and I'll remember it to my dying day, 'The innocent walk with God—that's why He don't get hurt.' " Whenever Mrs. Whipple repeated these words, she always felt a warm pool spread in her breast, and the tears would fill her eyes, and then she could talk about something else.

He did grow and He never got hurt. A plank blew off the chicken house and struck Him on the head and He never seemed to know it. He had learned a few words, and after this He forgot them. He didn't whine for food as the other children did, but waited until it was given Him; He ate squatting in the corner, smacking and mumbling. Rolls of fat covered Him like an overcoat, and He could carry twice as much wood and water as Adna. Emly had a cold in the head most of the time—"she takes that after me," said Mrs. Whipple—so in bad weather they gave her the extra blanket off His cot. He never seemed to mind the cold.

Just the same, Mrs. Whipple's life was a torment for fear something might happen to Him. He climbed the peach trees much better than Adna and went skittering along the branches like a monkey, just a regular monkey. "Oh, Mrs. Whipple, you hadn't ought to let Him do that. He'll lose His balance sometime. He can't rightly know what He's doing."

He

Mrs. Whipple almost screamed out at the neighbor. "He *does* know what He's doing! He's as able as any other child! Come down out of there, you!" When He finally reached the ground she could hardly keep her hands off Him for acting like that before people, a grin all over His face and her worried sick about Him all the time.

"It's the neighbors," said Mrs. Whipple to her husband. "Oh, I do mortally wish they would keep out of our business. I can't afford to let Him do anything for fear they'll come nosing around about it. Look at the bees, now. Adna can't handle them, they sting him up so; I haven't got time to do everything, and now I don't dare let Him. But if He gets a sting He don't really mind."

"It's just because He ain't got sense enough to be scared of anything," said Mr. Whipple.

"You ought to be ashamed of yourself," said Mrs. Whipple, "talking that way about your own child. Who's to take up for Him if we don't, I'd like to know? He sees a lot that goes on, He listens to things all the time. And anything I tell Him to do He does it. Don't never let anybody hear you say such things. They'd think you favored the other children over Him."

"Well, now I don't, and you know it, and what's the use of getting all worked up about it? You always think the worst of everything. Just let Him alone, He'll get along somehow. He gets plenty to eat and wear, don't He?" Mr. Whipple suddenly felt tired out. "Anyhow, it can't be helped now."

Mrs. Whipple felt tired too, she complained in a tired voice. "What's done can't never be undone, I know that good as anybody; but He's my child, and I'm not going to have people say anything. I get sick of people coming around saying things all the time."

In the early fall Mrs. Whipple got a letter from her brother saying he and his wife and two children were coming over for a little visit next Sunday week. "Put the big pot in the little one," he wrote at the end. Mrs. Whipple read this part out loud twice, she was so pleased. Her brother was a great one for saying funny things. "We'll just show him that's no joke," she said, "we'll just butcher one of the sucking pigs."

"It's a waste and I don't hold with waste the way we are now," said Mr. Whipple. "That pig'll be worth money by Christmas."

"It's a shame and a pity we can't have a decent meal's vittles once in a while when my own family comes to see us," said Mrs. Whipple. "I'd hate for his wife to go back and say there wasn't a thing in the house to eat. My God, it's better than buying up a great chance of meat in town. There's where you'd spend the money!"

He

"All right, do it yourself then," said Mr. Whipple. "Christamighty, no wonder we can't get ahead!"

The question was how to get the little pig away from his ma, a great fighter, worse than a Jersey cow. Adna wouldn't try it: "That sow'd rip my insides out all over the pen." "All right, old fraidy," said Mrs. Whipple, "*He's* not scared. Watch *Him* do it." And she laughed as though it was all a good joke and gave Him a little push towards the pen. He sneaked up and snatched the pig right away from the teat and galloped back and was over the fence with the sow raging at His heels. The little black squirming thing was screeching like a baby in a tantrum, stiffening its back and stretching its mouth to the ears. Mrs. Whipple took the pig with her face stiff and sliced its throat with one stroke. When He saw the blood He gave a great jolting breath and ran away. "But He'll forget and eat plenty, just the same," thought Mrs. Whipple. Whenever she was thinking, her lips moved making words. "He'd eat it all if I didn't stop Him. He'd eat up every mouthful from the other two if I'd let Him."

She felt badly about it. He was ten years old now and a third again as large as Adna, who was going on fourteen. "It's a shame, a shame," she kept saying under her breath, "and Adna with so much brains!"

She kept on feeling badly about all sorts of things.

In the first place it was the man's work to butcher; the sight of the pig scraped pink and naked made her sick. He was too fat and soft and pitiful-looking. It was simply a shame the way things had to happen. By the time she had finished it up, she almost wished her brother would stay at home.

Early Sunday morning Mrs. Whipple dropped everything to get Him all cleaned up. In an hour He was dirty again, with crawling under fences after a possum, and straddling along the rafters of the barn looking for eggs in the hayloft. "My Lord, look at you now after all my trying! And here's Adna and Emly staying so quiet. I get tired trying to keep you decent. Get off that shirt and put on another, people will say I don't half dress you!" And she boxed Him on the ears, hard. He blinked and blinked and rubbed His head, and His face hurt Mrs. Whipple's feelings. Her knees began to tremble, she had to sit down while she buttoned His shirt. "I'm just all gone before the day starts."

The brother came with his plump healthy wife and two great roaring hungry boys. They had a grand dinner, with the pig roasted to a crackling in the middle of the table, full of dressing, a pickled peach in his mouth and plenty of gravy for the sweet potatoes.

"This looks like prosperity all right," said the brother;

"you're going to have to roll me home like I was a barrel when I'm done."

Everybody laughed out loud; it was fine to hear them laughing all at once around the table. Mrs. Whipple felt warm and good about it. "Oh, we've got six more of these; I say it's as little as we can do when you come to see us so seldom."

He wouldn't come into the dining room, and Mrs. Whipple passed it off very well. "He's timider than my other two," she said, "He'll just have to get used to you. There isn't everybody He'll make up with, you know how it is with some children, even cousins." Nobody said anything out of the way.

"Just like my Alfy here," said the brother's wife. "I sometimes got to lick him to make him shake hands with his own grand-mammy."

So that was over, and Mrs. Whipple loaded up a big plate for Him first, before everybody. "I always say He ain't to be slighted, no matter who else goes without," she said, and carried it to Him herself.

"He can chin Himself on the top of the door," said Emly, helping along.

"That's fine, He's getting along fine," said the brother.

They went away after supper. Mrs. Whipple rounded up the dishes, and sent the children to bed and sat down and unlaced her shoes. "You see?" she said to Mr. Whipple. "That's the way my whole family is. Nice and considerate about everything. No out-of-the-way remarks—they *have* got refinement. I get awfully sick of people's remarks. Wasn't that pig good?"

Mr. Whipple said, "Yes, we're out three hundred pounds of pork, that's all. It's easy to be polite when you come to eat. Who knows what they had in their minds all along?"

"Yes, that's like you," said Mrs. Whipple. "I don't expect anything else from you. You'll be telling me next that my own brother will be saying around that we made Him eat in the kitchen! Oh, my God!" She rocked her head in her hands, a hard pain started in the very middle of her forehead. "Now it's all spoiled, and everything was so nice and easy. All right, you don't like them and you never did—all right, they'll not come here again soon, never you mind! But they *can't* say He wasn't dressed every lick as good as Adna—oh, honest, sometimes I wish I was dead!"

"I wish you'd let up," said Mr. Whipple. "It's bad enough as it is."

It was a hard winter. It seemed to Mrs. Whipple that they hadn't ever known anything but hard times, and now to cap it all a winter like this. The crops were about half of what they had a right to expect; after the cotton was in it didn't do much more than cover the grocery bill. They swapped off one of the plow horses, and got cheated, for the new one died of the heaves. Mrs. Whipple kept thinking all the time it was terrible to have a man you couldn't depend on not to get cheated. They cut down on everything, but Mrs. Whipple kept saying there are things you can't cut down on, and they cost money. It took a lot of warm clothes for Adna and Emly, who walked four miles to school during the three-months session. "He sets around the fire a lot, He won't need so much," said Mr. Whipple. "That's so," said Mrs. Whipple, "and when He does the outdoor chores He can wear your tarpaullion coat. I can't do no better, that's all."

In February He was taken sick, and lay curled up under His blanket looking very blue in the face and acting as if He would choke. Mr. and Mrs. Whipple did everything they could for Him for two days, and then they were scared and sent for the doctor. The doctor told them they must keep Him warm and give Him plenty of milk and eggs. "He isn't as stout as He looks, I'm afraid," said the doctor. "You've got to watch them when they're like that. You must put more cover onto Him, too."

"I just took off His big blanket to wash," said **Mrs.** Whipple, ashamed. "I can't stand dirt."

"Well, you'd better put it back on the minute it's dry," said the doctor, "or He'll have pneumonia."

Mr. and Mrs. Whipple took a blanket off their own bed and put His cot in by the fire. "They can't say we didn't do everything for Him," she said, "even to sleeping cold ourselves on His account."

When the winter broke He seemed to be well again, but He walked as if His feet hurt Him. He was able to run a cotton planter during the season.

"I got it all fixed up with Jim Ferguson about breeding the cow next time," said Mr. Whipple. "I'll pasture the bull this summer and give Jim some fodder in the fall. That's better than paying out money when you haven't got it."

"I hope you didn't say such a thing before Jim Ferguson," said Mrs. Whipple. "You oughtn't to let him know we're so down as all that."

"Godamighty, that ain't saying we're down. A man is got to look ahead sometimes. *He* can lead the bull over today. I need Adna on the place."

At first Mrs. Whipple felt easy in her mind about sending Him for the bull. Adna was too jumpy and couldn't be trusted. You've got to be steady around animals. After He was gone she started thinking, and

71

after a while she could hardly bear it any longer. She stood in the lane and watched for Him. It was nearly three miles to go and a hot day, but He oughtn't to be so long about it. She shaded her eyes and stared until colored bubbles floated in her eyeballs. It was just like everything else in life, she must always worry and never know a moment's peace about anything. After a long time she saw Him turn into the side lane, limping. He came on very slowly, leading the big hulk of an animal by a ring in the nose, twirling a little stick in His hand, never looking back or sideways, but coming on like a sleepwalker with His eyes half shut.

Mrs. Whipple was scared sick of bulls; she had heard awful stories about how they followed on quietly enough, and then suddenly pitched on with a bellow and pawed and gored a body to pieces. Any second now that black monster would come down on Him, my God, He'd never have sense enough to run.

She mustn't make a sound nor a move; she mustn't get the bull started. The bull heaved his head aside and horned the air at a fly. Her voice burst out of her in a shriek, and she screamed at Him to come on, for God's sake. He didn't seem to hear her clamor, but kept on twirling His switch and limping on, and the bull lumbered along behind him as gently as a calf. Mrs. Whipple stopped calling and ran towards the house, praying under her breath: "Lord, don't let anything happen to Him. Lord, you *know* people will say we oughtn't to have sent Him. You *know* they'll say we didn't take care of Him. Oh, get Him home, safe home, safe home, and I'll look out for Him better! Amen."

She watched from the window while He led the beast in, and tied him up in the barn. It was no use trying to keep up, Mrs. Whipple couldn't bear another thing. She sat down and rocked and cried with her apron over her head.

From year to year the Whipples were growing poorer and poorer. The place just seemed to run down of itself, no matter how hard they worked. "We're losing our hold," said Mrs. Whipple. "Why can't we do like other people and watch for our best chances? They'll be calling us poor white trash next."

"When I get to be sixteen I'm going to leave," said Adna. "I'm going to get a job in Powell's grocery store. There's money in that. No more farm for me."

"I'm going to be a schoolteacher," said Emly. "But I've got to finish the eighth grade, anyhow. Then I can live in town. I don't see any chances here."

"Emly takes after my family," said Mrs. Whipple. "Ambitious every last one of them, and they don't take second place for anybody."

73

He

When fall came Emly got a chance to wait on table in the railroad eating-house in the town near by, and it seemed such a shame not to take it when the wages were good and she could get her food too, that Mrs. Whipple decided to let her take it, and not bother with school until the next session. "You've got plenty of time," she said. "You're young and smart as a whip."

With Adna gone too, Mr. Whipple tried to run the farm with just Him to help. He seemed to get along fine, doing His work and part of Adna's without noticing it. They did well enough until Christmas time, when one morning He slipped on the ice coming up from the barn. Instead of getting up He thrashed round and round, and when Mr. Whipple got to Him, He was having some sort of fit.

They brought Him inside and tried to make Him sit up, but He blubbered and rolled, so they put Him to bed and Mr. Whipple rode to town for the doctor. All the way there and back he worried about where the money was to come from: it sure did look like he had about all the troubles he could carry.

From then on He stayed in bed. His legs swelled up double their size, and the fits kept coming back. After four months, the doctor said, "It's no use, I think you'd better put Him in the County Home for treatment right away. I'll see about it for you. He'll have good care there and be off your hands."

"We don't begrudge Him any care, and I won't let Him out of my sight," said Mrs. Whipple. "I won't have it said I sent my sick child off among strangers."

"I know how you feel," said the doctor. "You can't tell me anything about that, Mrs. Whipple. I've got a boy of my own. But you'd better listen to me. I can't do anything more for Him, that's the truth."

Mr. and Mrs. Whipple talked it over a long time that night after they went to bed. "It's just charity," said Mrs. Whipple, "that's what we've come to, charity! I certainly never looked for this."

"We pay taxes to help support the place just like everybody else," said Mr. Whipple, "and I don't call that taking charity. I think it would be fine to have Him where He'd get the best of everything . . . and be-sides, I can't keep up with these doctor bills any longer."

"Maybe that's why the doctor wants us to send Him—he's scared he won't get his money," said Mrs. Whipple.

"Don't talk like that," said Mr. Whipple, feeling pretty sick, "or we won't be able to send Him."

"Oh, but we won't keep Him there long," said Mrs. Whipple. "Soon's He's better, we'll bring Him right back home."

"The doctor has told you and told you time and again He can't ever get better, and you might as well stop talking," said Mr. Whipple.

"Doctors don't know everything," said Mrs. Whipple, feeling almost happy. "But anyhow, in the summer Emly can come home for a vacation, and Adna can get down for Sundays: we'll all work together and get on our feet again, and the children will feel they've got a place to come to."

All at once she saw it full summer again, with the garden going fine, and new white roller shades up all over the house, and Adna and Emly home, so full of life, all of them happy together. Oh, it could happen, things would ease up on them.

They didn't talk before Him much, but they never knew just how much He understood. Finally the doctor set the day and a neighbor who owned a double-seated carryall offered to drive them over. The hospital would have sent an ambulance, but Mrs. Whipple couldn't stand to see Him going away looking so sick as all that. They wrapped Him in blankets, and the neighbor and Mr. Whipple lifted Him into the back seat of the carryall beside Mrs. Whipple, who had on her black shirtwaist. She couldn't stand to go looking like charity.

"You'll be all right, I guess I'll stay behind," said Mr.

Whipple. "It don't look like everybody ought to leave the place at once."

"Besides, it ain't as if He was going to stay forever," said Mrs. Whipple to the neighbor. "This is only for a little while."

They started away, Mrs. Whipple holding to the edges of the blankets to keep Him from sagging sideways. He sat there blinking and blinking. He worked His hands out and began rubbing His nose with His knuckles, and then with the end of the blanket. Mrs. Whipple couldn't believe what she saw; He was scrubbing away big tears that rolled out of the corners of His eyes. He sniveled and made a gulping noise. Mrs. Whipple kept saying, "Oh, honey, you don't feel so bad, do you? You don't feel so bad, do you?" for He seemed to be accusing her of something. Maybe He remembered that time she boxed His ears, maybe He had been scared that day with the bull, maybe He had slept cold and couldn't tell her about it; maybe He knew they were sending Him away for good and all because they were too poor to keep Him. Whatever it was, Mrs. Whipple couldn't bear to think of it. She began to cry, frightfully, and wrapped her arms tight around Him. His head rolled on her shoulder: she had loved Him as much as she possibly could, there were Adna and Emly who had to be thought of too, there was nothing she could do to make up to

Him for His life. Oh, what a mortal pity He was ever born.

They came in sight of the hospital, with the neighbor driving very fast, not daring to look behind him.

THEFT

Theft

SHE had the purse in her hand when she came in. Standing in the middle of the floor, holding her bathrobe around her and trailing a damp towel in one hand, she surveyed the immediate past and remembered everything clearly. Yes, she had opened the flap and spread it out on the bench after she had dried the purse with her handkerchief.

She had intended to take the Elevated, and naturally she looked in her purse to make certain she had the fare, and was pleased to find forty cents in the coin envelope. She was going to pay her own fare, too, even if Camilo did have the habit of seeing her up the steps and dropping a nickel in the machine before he gave the turnstile a little push and sent her through it with a bow. Camilo by a series of compromises had managed to make effective a fairly complete set of smaller courtesies, ignoring the larger and more troublesome ones. She had walked with him to the station in a pouring rain, because she knew he was almost as poor as she was, and when he insisted on a taxi, she was firm and said, "You know it simply will not do." He was wearing a new hat of a pretty biscuit shade, for it never occurred to him to buy anything of a practical color; he had put it on for the first time and the rain was spoiling it. She kept thinking, "But this is dreadful, where will he get another?" She compared it with Eddie's hats that always seemed to be precisely seven years old and as if they had been quite purposely left out in the rain, and yet they sat with a careless and incidental rightness on Eddie. But Camilo was far different; if he wore a shabby hat it would be merely shabby on him, and he would lose his spirits over it. If she had not feared Camilo would take it badly, for he insisted on the practice of his little ceremonies up to the point he had fixed for them, she would have said to him as they left Thora's house, "Do go home. I can surely reach the station by myself."

"It is written that we must be rained upon tonight," said Camilo, "so let it be together."

At the foot of the platform stairway she staggered slightly—they were both nicely set up on Thora's cocktails—and said: "At least, Camilo, do me the favor not to climb these stairs in your present state, since for you it is only a matter of coming down again at once, and you'll certainly break your neck."

He made three quick bows, he was Spanish, and leaped off through the rainy darkness. She stood watching him, for he was a very graceful young man, thinking that tomorrow morning he would gaze soberly at his spoiled hat and soggy shoes and possibly associate her with his misery. As she watched, he stopped at the far corner and took off his hat and hid it under his over-coat. She felt she had betrayed him by seeing, because he would have been humiliated if he thought she even sus-pected him of trying to save his hat.

Roger's voice sounded over her shoulder above the clang of the rain falling on the stairway shed, wanting to know what she was doing out in the rain at this time of night, and did she take herself for a duck? His long, imperturbable face was streaming with water, and he tapped a bulging spot on the breast of his buttoned-up overcoat: "Hat," he said. "Come on, let's take a taxi."

She settled back against Roger's arm which he laid around her shoulders, and with the gesture they ex-changed a glance full of long amiable associations, then she looked through the window at the rain changing the shapes of everything, and the colors. The taxi dodged in and out between the pillars of the Elevated, skidding slightly on every curve, and she said: "The more it skids the calmer I feel, so I really must be drunk."

"You must be," said Roger. "This bird is a homicidal maniac, and I could do with a cocktail myself this minute."

They waited on the traffic at Fortieth Street and Sixth

Avenue, and three boys walked before the nose of the taxi. Under the globes of light they were cheerful scarecrows, all very thin and all wearing very seedy snappy-cut suits and gay neckties. They were not very sober either, and they stood for a moment wobbling in front of the car, and there was an argument going on among them. They leaned toward each other as if they were getting ready to sing, and the first one said: "When I get married it won't be jus' for getting married, I'm gonna marry for *love*, see?" and the second one said, "Aw, gwan and tell that stuff to *her*, why n't yuh?" and the third one gave a kind of hoot, and said, "Hell, dis guy? Wot the hell's he got?" and the first one said: "Aaah, shurrup yuh mush, I got plenty." Then they all squealed and scrambled across the street beating the first one on the back and pushing him around.

"Nuts," commented Roger, "pure nuts."

Two girls went skittering by in short transparent raincoats, one green, one red, their heads tucked against the drive of the rain. One of them was saying to the other, "Yes, I know all about *that*. But what about me? You're always so sorry for *him* . . ." and they ran on with their little pelican legs flashing back and forth.

The taxi backed up suddenly and leaped forward again, and after a while Roger said: "I had a letter from Stella today, and she'll be home on the twenty-sixth, so

I suppose she's made up her mind and it's all settled."

"I had a sort of letter today too," she said, "making up my mind for me. I think it is time for you and Stella to do something definite."

When the taxi stopped on the corner of West Fifty-third Street, Roger said, "I've just enough if you'll add ten cents," so she opened her purse and gave him a dime, and he said, "That's beautiful, that purse."

"It's a birthday present," she told him, "and I like it. How's your show coming?"

"Oh, still hanging on, I guess. I don't go near the place. Nothing sold yet. I mean to keep right on the way I'm going and they can take it or leave it. I'm through with the argument."

"It's absolutely a matter of holding out, isn't it?"

"Holding out's the tough part."

"Good night, Roger."

"Good night, you should take aspirin and push yourself into a tub of hot water, you look as though you're catching cold."

"I will."

With the purse under her arm she went upstairs, and on the first landing Bill heard her step and poked his head out with his hair tumbled and his eyes red, and he said: "For Christ's sake, come in and have a drink with me. I've had some bad news."

"You're perfectly sopping," said Bill, looking at her drenched feet. They had two drinks, while Bill told how the director had thrown his play out after the cast had been picked over twice, and had gone through three rehearsals. "I said to him, 'I didn't say it was a masterpiece, I said it would make a good show.' And he said, 'It just doesn't *play*, do you see? It needs a doctor.' So I'm stuck, absolutely stuck," said Bill, on the edge of weeping again. "I've been crying," he told her, "in my cups." And he went on to ask her if she realized his wife was ruining him with her extravagance. "I send her ten dollars every week of my unhappy life, and I don't really have to. She threatens to jail me if I don't, but she can't do it. God, let her try it after the way she treated me! She's no right to alimony and she knows it. She keeps on saying she's got to have it for the baby and I keep on sending it because I can't bear to see anybody suffer. So I'm way behind on the piano and the victrola, both—"

"Well, this is a pretty rug, anyhow," she said.

Bill stared at it and blew his nose. "I got it at Ricci's for ninety-five dollars," he said. "Ricci told me it once belonged to Marie Dressler, and cost fifteen hundred dollars, but there's a burnt place on it, under the divan. Can you beat that?"

"No," she said. She was thinking about her empty purse and that she could not possibly expect a check for her latest review for another three days, and her arrangement with the basement restaurant could not last much longer if she did not pay something on account. "It's no time to speak of it," she said, "but I've been hoping you would have by now that fifty dollars you promised for my scene in the third act. Even if it doesn't play. You were to pay me for the work anyhow out of your advance."

"Weeping Jesus," said Bill, "you, too?" He gave a loud sob, or hiccough, in his moist handkerchief. "Your stuff was no better than mine, after all. Think of that."

"But you got something for it," she said. "Seven hundred dollars."

Bill said, "Do me a favor, will you? Have another drink and forget about it. I can't, you know I can't, I would if I could, but you know the fix I'm in."

"Let it go, then," she found herself saying almost in spite of herself. She had meant to be quite firm about it. They drank again without speaking, and she went to her apartment on the floor above.

There, she now remembered distinctly, she had taken the letter out of the purse before she spread the purse out to dry.

She had sat down and read the letter over again: but there were phrases that insisted on being read many times, they had a life of their own separate from the

87

others, and when she tried to read past and around them, they moved with the movement of her eyes, and she could not escape them . . . "thinking about you more than I mean to . . . yes, I even talk about you . . . why were you so anxious to destroy . . . even if I could see you now I would not . . . not worth all this abominable . . . the end . . ."

Carefully she tore the letter into narrow strips and touched a lighted match to them in the coal grate.

Early the next morning she was in the bathtub when the janitress knocked and then came in, calling out that she wished to examine the radiators before she started the furnace going for the winter. After moving about the room for a few minutes, the janitress went out, closing the door very sharply.

She came out of the bathroom to get a cigarette from the package in the purse. The purse was gone. She dressed and made coffee, and sat by the window while she drank it. Certainly the janitress had taken the purse, and certainly it would be impossible to get it back without a great deal of ridiculous excitement. Then let it go. With this decision of her mind, there rose coincidentally in her blood a deep almost murderous anger. She set the cup carefully in the center of the table, and walked steadily downstairs, three long flights and a short hall and a steep short flight into the basement, where the janitress, her face streaked with coal dust, was shaking up the furnace. "Will you please give me back my purse? There isn't any money in it. It was a present, and I don't want to lose it."

The janitress turned without straightening up and peered at her with hot flickering eyes, a red light from the furnace reflected in them. "What do you mean, your purse?"

"The gold cloth purse you took from the wooden bench in my room," she said. "I must have it back."

"Before God I never laid eyes on your purse, and that's the holy truth," said the janitress.

"Oh, well then, keep it," she said, but in a very bitter voice; "keep it if you want it so much." And she walked away.

She remembered how she had never locked a door in her life, on some principle of rejection in her that made her uncomfortable in the ownership of things, and her paradoxical boast before the warnings of her friends, that she had never lost a penny by theft; and she had been pleased with the bleak humility of this concrete example designed to illustrate and justify a certain fixed, otherwise baseless and general faith which ordered the movements of her life without regard to her will in the matter.

In this moment she felt that she had been robbed

of an enormous number of valuable things, whether material or intangible: things lost or broken by her own fault, things she had forgotten and left in houses when she moved: books borrowed from her and not returned, journeys she had planned and had not made, words she had waited to hear spoken to her and had not heard, and the words she had meant to answer with; bitter alternatives and intolerable substitutes worse than nothing, and yet inescapable: the long patient suffering of dying friendships and the dark inexplicable death of love—all that she had had, and all that she had missed, were lost together, and were twice lost in this landslide of remembered losses.

The janitress was following her upstairs with the purse in her hand and the same deep red fire flickering in her eyes. The janitress thrust the purse towards her while they were still a half dozen steps apart, and said: "Don't never tell on me. I musta been crazy. I get crazy in the head sometimes, I swear I do. My son can tell you."

She took the purse after a moment, and the janitress went on: "I got a niece who is going on seventeen, and she's a nice girl and I thought I'd give it to her. She needs a pretty purse. I musta been crazy; I thought maybe you wouldn't mind, you leave things around and don't seem to notice much."

She said: "I missed this because it was a present to me from someone . . ."

The janitress said: "He'd get you another if you lost this one. My niece is young and needs pretty things, we oughta give the young ones a chance. She's got young men after her maybe will want to marry her. She oughta have nice things. She needs them bad right now. You're a grown woman, you've had your chance, you ought to know how it is!"

She held the purse out to the janitress saying: "You don't know what you're talking about. Here, take it, I've changed my mind. I really don't want it."

The janitress looked up at her with hatred and said: "I don't want it either now. My niece is young and pretty, she don't need fixin' up to be pretty, she's young and pretty anyhow! I guess you need it worse than she does!"

"It wasn't really yours in the first place," she said, turning away. "You mustn't talk as if I had stolen it from you."

"It's not from me, it's from her you're stealing it," said the janitress, and went back downstairs.

She laid the purse on the table and sat down with the cup of chilled coffee, and thought: I was right not to be afraid of any thief but myself, who will end by leaving me nothing.

THAT TREE

That Tree

HE had really wanted to be a cheerful bum lying under a tree in a good climate, writing poetry. He wrote bushel basketsful of poetry and it was all no good and he knew it, even while he was writing it. Knowing his poetry was no good did not take away much from his pleasure in it. He would have enjoyed just that kind of life: no respectability, no responsibility, no money to speak of, wearing worn-out sandals and a becoming, if probably ragged, blue shirt, lying under a tree writing poetry. That was why he had come to Mexico in the first place. He had felt in his bones that it was the country for him. Long after he had become quite an important journalist, an authority on Latin-American revolutions and a best seller, he confessed to any friends and acquaintances who would listen to him—he enjoyed this confession, it gave him a chance to talk about the thing he believed he loved best, the idle free romantic life of a poet—that the day Miriam kicked him out was the luckiest day of his life. She had left him, really, packing up suddenly in a cold quiet fury, stabbing him with her elbows when he tried to get his arms around her, now and again cutting him to the bone with a short sentence expelled through her clenched teeth; but he felt that he had been, as he always explained, kicked out. She had kicked him out and it had served him right.

The shock had brought him to himself as if he had been surprised out of a long sleep. He had sat quite benumbed in the bare clean room, among the straw mats and the painted Indian chairs Miriam hated, in the sudden cold silence, his head in his hands, nearly all night. It hadn't even occurred to him to lie down. It must have been almost daylight when he got up stiff in every joint from sitting still so long, and though he could not say he had been thinking yet he had formed a new resolution. He had started out, you might almost say that very day, to make a career for himself in journalism. He couldn't say why he had hit on that, except that the word would impress his wife, the work was just intellectual enough to save his self-respect, such as it was, and even to him it seemed a suitable occupation for a man such as he had suddenly become, bent on getting on in the world of affairs. Nothing ever happens suddenly to anyone, he observed, as if the thought had just occurred to him; it had been coming on probably for a long time, sneaking up on him when he wasn't looking. His wife had called him "Parasite!" She had said "Ne'er-do-well!" and as she repeated these things for what proved to be the last time, it struck him she had said them often before, when he had not listened to her with the ear of his mind. He translated these relatively harmless epithets instantly into their proper synonyms of Loafer! and Bum! Miriam had been a schoolteacher, and no matter what her disappointments and provocations may have been, you could not expect her easily to forget such discipline. She had got into a professional habit of primness; besides, she was a properly brought-up girl, not a prissy bore, not at all, but a—well, there you are, a nicely brought-up Middle-Western girl, who took life seriously. And what can you do about that? She was sweet and gay and full of little crazy notions, but she never gave way to them honestly, or at least never at the moment when they might have meant something. She was never able to see the amusing side of a threatening situation which, taken solemnly, would ruin everything. No, her sense of humor never worked for salvation. It was just an extra frill on what would have been a good time anyhow.

He wondered if anybody had ever thought—oh, well, of course everybody else had, he was always making marvelous discoveries that other people had known all along—how impossible it is to explain or to make other eyes see the special qualities in the person you love. There was such a special kind of beauty in Miriam. In certain lights and moods he simply got a clutch in the pit of his stomach when he looked at her. It was something that could happen at any hour of the day, in the midst of the most ordinary occupations. He thought there was something to be said for living with one person day and night the year round. It brings out the worst, but it brings out the best, too, and Miriam's best was pretty damn swell. He couldn't describe it. It was easy to talk about her faults. He remembered all of them, he could add them up against her like rows of figures in a vast unpaid debt. He had lived with her for four years, and even now sometimes he woke out of a sound sleep in a sweating rage with himself, asking himself again why he had ever wasted a minute on her. She wasn't beautiful in his style. He confessed to a weakness for the kind that knocks your eye out. Her notion of daytime dress was a tailored suit with a round-collared blouse and a little felt hat like a bent shovel pulled down over her eyes. In the evening she put on a black dinner dress, positively disappeared into it. But she did her hair well and had the most becoming nightgowns he ever saw. You could have put her mind in a peanut shell. She hadn't temperament of the kind he had got used to in the Mexican girls. She did not approve of his use of the word temperament, either. She thought it was a kind of occupational disease among artists, or a trick they practiced to make themselves interesting. In any case, she distrusted artists and she distrusted temperament. But there was something about her. In cold blood he could size her up to himself, but it made him furious if anyone even hinted a criticism against her. His second wife had made a point of being catty about Miriam. In the end he could almost be willing to say this had led to his second divorce. He could not bear hearing Miriam called a mousy little nit-wit—at least not by *that* woman . . .

They both jumped nervously at an explosion in the street, the backfire of an automobile.

"Another revolution," said the fat scarlet young man in the tight purplish suit, at the next table. He looked like a parboiled sausage ready to burst from its skin. It was the oldest joke since the Mexican Independence, but he was trying to look as if he had invented it. The journalist glanced back at him over a sloping shoulder. "Another of those smart-cracking newspaper guys," he said in a tough voice, too loudly on purpose, "sitting around the Hotel Regis lobby wearing out the spittoons."

The smart-cracker swelled visibly and turned a darker red. "Who do you think you're talking about, you banjo-eyed chinless wonder, you?" he asked explicitly, spreading his chest across the table.

"Somebody way up, no doubt." said the journalist, in

99

his natural voice, "somebody in with the government, I'll bet."

"Dyuhwana fight?" asked the newspaper man, trying to unwedge himself from between the table and his chair, which sat against the wall.

"Oh, I don't mind," said the journalist, "if you don't."

The newspaper man's friends laid soothing paws all over him and held him down. "Don't start anything with that shrimp," said one of them, his wet pink eyes trying to look sober and responsible. "For crisesake, Joe, can't you see he's about half your size and a feeb to boot? You wouldn't hit a feeb, now, Joe, would you?"

"I'll feeb him," said the newspaper man, wiggling faintly under restraint.

"*Señores'n, señores'n,*" urged the little Mexican waiter, "there are respectable ladies and gentlemen present. Please, a little silence and correct behavior, please."

"Who the hell are *you*, anyhow?" the newspaper man asked the journalist, from under his shelter of hands, around the thin form of the waiter.

"Nobody you'd wanta know, Joe," said another of his pawing friends. "Pipe down now before these greasers turn in a general alarm. You know how liable they are to go off when you least expect it. Pipe down, now, Joe, now you just remember what happened the last time, Joe. Whaddayah *care*, anyhow?"

"*Señores'n*," said the little waiter, working his thin outspread mahogany-colored hands up and down alternately as if they were on sticks, "it is necessary it must cease or the *señores'n* must remove themselves."

It did cease. It seemed to evaporate. The four newspaper men at the next table subsided, cluttered in a circle with their heads together, muttering into their highballs. The journalist turned back, ordered another round of drinks, and went on talking, in a low voice.

He had never liked this café, never had any luck in it. Something always happened here to spoil his evening. If there was one brand of bum on earth he despised, it was a newspaper bum. Or anyhow the drunken illiterates the United Press and Associated Press seemed to think were good enough for Mexico and South America. They were always getting mixed up in affairs that were none of their business, and they spent their time trying to work up trouble somewhere so they could get a story out of it. They were always having to be thrown out on their ears by the government. He just happened to know that the bum at the next table was about due to be deported. It had been pretty safe to make that crack about how he was no doubt way up in Mexican official esteem. . . . He thought that would remind him of something, all right.

One evening he had come here with Miriam for dinner and dancing, and at the very next table sat four fat generals from the North, with oxhorn mustaches and big bellies and big belts full of cartridges and pistols. It was in the old days just after Obregón had taken the city, and the town was crawling with generals. They infested the steam baths, where they took off their soiled campaign harness and sweated away the fumes of tequila and fornication, and they infested the cafés to get drunk again on champagne, and pick up the French whores who had been imported for the festivities of the presidential inauguration. These four were having an argument very quietly, their mean little eyes boring into each other's faces. He and his wife were dancing within arm's length of the table when one of the generals got up suddenly, tugging at his pistol, which stuck, and the other three jumped and grabbed him, all without a word; everybody in the place saw it at once. So far there was nothing unusual. The point was, every right-minded Mexican girl just seized her man firmly by the waist and spun him around until his back was to the generals, holding him before her like a shield, and there the whole roomful had stood frozen for a second, the music dead. His wife Miriam had broken from him and hidden under a table. He had to drag her out by the arm before everybody. "Let's have another drink," he said, and paused, looking around him as if he saw again the place as it had been on that night nearly ten years before. He blinked, and went on. It had been the most utterly humiliating moment of his whole blighted life. He had thought he couldn't survive to pick up their things and get her out of there. The generals had all sat down again and everybody went on dancing as though nothing had happened. . . . Indeed, nothing had happened to anyone except himself.

He tried, for hours that night and on and on for nearly a year, to explain to her how he felt about it. She could not understand at all. Sometimes she said it was all perfect nonsense. Or she remarked complacently that it had never occurred to her to save her life at his expense. She thought such tricks were all very well for the Mexican girls who had only one idea in their heads, and any excuse would do to hold a man closer than they should, but she could not, could *not*, see why he should expect her to imitate them. Besides, she had felt safer under the table. It was her first and only thought. He told her a bullet might very well have gone through the wood; a plank was no protection at all, a human torso was as good as a feather pillow to stop a bullet. She kept saying it simply had not occurred to her to do anything else, and that it really had nothing at all to do with him. He could never make her see his point of view for one moment. It should have had something to do with him.

All those Mexican girls were born knowing what they should do and they did it instantly, and Miriam had merely proved once for all that her instincts were out of tune. When she tightened her mouth to bite her lip and say "Instincts!" she could make it sound like the most obscene word in any language. It was a shocking word. And she did not stop there. At last she said, she hadn't the faintest interest in what Mexican girls were born for, but she had no intention of wasting her life flattering male vanity. "Why should I trust you in anything?" she asked. "What reason have you given me to trust you?"

He was surprised at the change in her since he had first met her in Minneapolis. He chose to believe this change had been caused by her teaching school. He told her he thought it the most deadly occupation there was and a law should be passed prohibiting pretty women under thirty-five years of age from taking it up. She reminded him they were living on the money she had earned at it. They had been engaged for three years, a chaste long-distance engagement which he considered morbid and unnatural. Of course he had to do something to wear away the time, so while she was in Minneapolis saving her money and filling a huge trunk with household linen, he had been living in Mexico City with an Indian girl who posed for a set of painters he knew. He

had a job teaching English in one of the technical schools
—damned odd, he had been a schoolteacher too, but he
never thought of it just that way until this minute—and
he lived very comfortably with the Indian girl on his
wages, for naturally the painters did not pay her for
posing. The Indian girl divided her time cheerfully between the painters, the cooking pot, and his bed, and she
managed to have a baby without interrupting any of
these occupations for more than a few days. Later on
she was taken up by one of the more famous and successful painters, and grew very sophisticated and a "character," but at that time she was still simple and nice.
She took, later on, to wearing native art-jewelry and
doing native dances in costume, and learned to paint
almost as well as a seven-year-old child; "you know,"
he said, "the primitive style." Well, by that time, he was
having troubles of his own. When the time came for
Miriam to come out and marry him—the whole delay,
he realized afterward, was caused by Miriam's expansive
notions of what a bride's outfit should be—the Indian
girl had gone away very cheerfully, too cheerfully, in
fact, with a new man. She had come back in three days
to say she was at last going to get married honestly,
and she felt he should give her the furniture for a dowry.
He had helped her pile the stuff on the backs of two
Indian carriers, and the girl had walked away with the

baby's head dangling out of her shawl. For just a moment when he saw the baby's face, he had an odd feeling. "That's mine," he said to himself, and added at once, "perhaps." There was no way of knowing, and it certainly looked like any other little shock-haired Indian baby. Of course the girl had not got married; she had never even thought of it.

When Miriam arrived, the place was almost empty, because he had not been able to save a peso. He had a bed and a stove, and the walls were decorated with drawings and paintings by his Mexican friends, and there was a litter of painted gourds and carved wood and pottery in beautiful colors. It didn't seem so bad to him, but Miriam's face, when she stepped into the first room, was, he had to admit, pretty much of a study. She said very little, but she began to be unhappy about a number of things. She cried intermittently for the first few weeks, for the most mysterious and far-fetched causes. He would wake in the night and find her crying hopelessly. When she sat down to coffee in the morning she would lean her head on her hands and cry. "It's nothing, nothing really," she would tell him. "I don't know what is the matter. I just want to cry." He knew now what was the matter. She had come all that way to marry after three years' planning, and she couldn't see herself going back and facing the music at home. This mood had not

lasted, but it made a fairly dreary failure of their honey-
moon. She knew nothing about the Indian girl, and believed, or professed to believe, that he was virgin as she
was at their marriage. She hadn't much curiosity and
her moral standards were severe, so it was impossible
for him ever to take her into his confidence about his
past. She simply took it for granted in the most irritating
way that he hadn't any past worth mentioning except
the three years they were engaged, and that, of course,
they shared already. He had believed that all virgins,
however austere their behavior, were palpitating to
learn about life, were you might say hanging on by an
eyelash until they arrived safely at initiation within the
secure yet libertine advantages of marriage. Miriam upset
this theory as in time she upset most of his theories. His
intention to play the rôle of a man of the world educat-
ing an innocent but interestingly teachable bride was
nipped in the bud. She was not at all teachable and she
took no trouble to make herself interesting. In their most
intimate hours her mind seemed elsewhere, gone into
some darkness of its own, as if a prior and greater shock
of knowledge had forestalled her attention. She was not
to be won, for reasons of her own which she would not
or could not give. He could not even play the rôle of
a poet. She was not interested in his poetry. She pre-
ferred Milton, and she let him know it. She let him know

also that she believed their mutual sacrifice of virginity
was the most important act of their marriage, and this
sacred rite once achieved, the whole affair had descended
to a pretty low plane. She had a terrible phrase about
"walking the chalk line" which she applied to all sorts
of situations. One walked, as never before, the chalk line
in marriage; there seemed to be a chalk line drawn between them as they lay together. . . .

The thing that finally got him down was Miriam's
devilish inconsistency. She spent three mortal years writing him how dull and dreadful and commonplace her life
was, how sick and tired she was of petty little conven-
tions and amusements, how narrow-minded everybody
around her was, how she longed to live in a beautiful
dangerous place among interesting people who painted
and wrote poetry, and how his letters came into her
stuffy little world like a breath of free mountain air, and
all that. "For God's sake," he said to his guest, "let's have
another drink." Well, he had something of a notion he
was freeing a sweet bird from a cage. Once freed, she
would perch gratefully on his hand. He wrote a poem
about a caged bird set free, dedicated it to her and sent
her a copy. She forgot to mention it in her next letter.
Then she came out with a two-hundred-pound trunk
of linen and enough silk underwear to last her a lifetime,
you might have supposed, expecting to settle down in

a modern steam-heated flat and have nice artistic young couples from the American colony in for dinner Wednesday evenings. No wonder her face had changed at the first glimpse of her new home. His Mexican friends had scattered flowers all over the place, tied bunches of carnations on the door knobs, almost carpeted the floor with red roses, pinned posies of small bright blooms on the sagging cotton curtains, spread a coverlet of gardenias on the lumpy bed, and had disappeared discreetly, leaving gay reassuring messages scribbled here and there, even on the white plastered walls. . . . She had walked through with a vague look of terror in her eyes, pushing back the wilting flowers with her advancing feet. She swept the gardenias aside to sit on the edge of the bed, and she had said not a word. Hail, Hymen! What next?

He had lost his teaching job almost immediately. The Minister of Education, who was a patron of the school superintendent, was put out of office suddenly, and naturally every soul in his party down to the school janitors went out with him, and there you were. After a while you learn to take such things calmly. You wait until your man gets back in the saddle or you work up an alliance with the new one. . . . Whichever . . . Meanwhile the change and movement made such a good show you almost forgot the effect it had on your food supply. Miriam was not interested in politics or the movement of local history. She could see nothing but that he had lost his job. They lived on Miriam's savings eked out with birthday checks and Christmas checks from her father, who threatened constantly to come for a visit, in spite of Miriam's desperate letters warning him that the country was appalling, and the climate would most certainly ruin his health. Miriam went on holding her nose when she went to the markets, trying to cook wholesome civilized American food over a charcoal brasier, and doing the washing in the patio over a stone tub with a cold water tap; and everything that had seemed so jolly and natural and inexpensive with the Indian girl was too damnifying and costly for words with Miriam. Her money melted away and they got nothing for it.

She would not have an Indian servant near her: they were dirty and besides how could she afford it? He could not see why she despised and resented housework so, especially since he offered to help. He had thought it rather a picnic to wash a lot of gayly colored Indian crockery outdoors in the sunshine, with the bouginvillea climbing up the wall and the heaven tree in full bloom. Not Miriam. She despised him for thinking it a picnic. He remembered for the first time his mother doing the housework when he was a child. There were half a dozen assorted children, her work was hard and endless, but she went about it with a quiet certainty, a happy absorbed look on her face, as if her hands were working automatically while her imagination was away playing somewhere. "Ah, your mother," said his wife, without any particular emphasis. He felt horribly injured, as if she were insulting his mother and calling down a curse on her head for bringing such a son into the world. No doubt about it, Miriam had force. She could make her personality, which no one need really respect, felt in a bitter, sinister way. She had a background, and solid earth under her feet, and a point of view and a strong spine: even when she danced with him he could feel her tense controlled hips and her locked knees, which gave her dancing a most attractive strength and lightness without any yielding at all. She had her points, all right, like a good horse, but she had missed being beautiful. It wasn't in her. He began to cringe when she reminded him that if he were an invalid she would cheerfully work for him and take care of him, but he appeared to be in the best of health, he was not even looking for a job, and he was still writing that poetry, which was the last straw. She called him a failure. She called him worthless and shiftless and trifling and faithless. She showed him her ruined hands and asked him what she had to look forward to, and told him again, and again, that she was not used to associating with the simply indescribably savage and awful persons who kept

streaming through the place. Moreover, she had no intention of getting used to it. He tried to tell her that these
persons were the best painters and poets and what-alls in
Mexico, that she should try to appreciate them; these
were the artists he had told her about in his letters. She
wanted to know why Carlos never changed his shirt.
"I told her," said the journalist, "it was because probably
he hadn't got any other shirt." And why was Jaime such
a glutton, leaning over his plate and wolfing his food?
Because he was famished, no doubt. It was precisely that
she could not understand. Why didn't they go to work
and make a living? It was no good trying to explain to
her his Franciscan notions of holy Poverty as being the
natural companion for the artist. She said, "So you
think they're being poor on purpose? Nobody but you
would be such a fool." Really, the things that girl said.
And his general impression of her was that she was silent
as a cat. He went on in his pawky way trying to make
clear to her his mystical faith in these men who went
ragged and hungry because they had chosen once for
all between what he called in all seriousness their souls,
and this world. Miriam knew better. She knew they were
looking for the main chance. "She was abominably, ob-
scenely right. How I hate that woman, I hate her as I
hate no one else. She assured me they were not so stupid
as I thought; and I lived to see Jaime take up with a rich

old woman, and Ricardo decide to turn film actor, and Carlos sitting easy with a government job, painting revolutionary frescoes to order, and I asked myself, Why shouldn't a man survive in any way he can?" But some fixed point of feeling in him refused to be convinced, he had a sackful of romantic notions about artists and their destiny and he was left holding it. Miriam had seen through them with half an eye, and how he wished he might have thought of a trick to play on her that would have finished her for life. But he had not. They all in turn ran out on him and in the end he had run out too. "So you see, I don't feel any better about doing what I did finally do, but I can say I am not unusual. That I can say. The trouble was that Miriam was right, damn her. I am not a poet, my poetry is filthy, and I had notions about artists that I must have got out of books. . . . You know, a race apart, dedicated men much superior to common human needs and ambitions. . . . I mean I thought art was a religion. . . . I mean that when Miriam kept saying . . ."

What he meant was that all this conflict began to damage him seriously. Miriam had become an avenging fury, yet he could not condemn her. Hate her, yes, that was almost too simple. His old-fashioned respectable middle-class hard-working American ancestry and training rose up in him and fought on Miriam's side. He felt he had broken about every bone in him to get away from them and live them down, and here he had been overtaken at last and beaten into resignation that had nothing to do with his mind or heart. It was as if his blood stream had betrayed him. The prospect of taking a job and being a decent little clerk with shiny pants and elbows—for he couldn't think of a job in any other terms—seemed like a kind of premature death which would not even compensate him with loss of memory. He didn't do anything about it at all. He did odd jobs and picked up a little money, but never enough. He could see her side of it, at least he tried hard to see it. When it came to a showdown, he hadn't a single argument in favor of his way of life that would hold water. He had been trying to live and think in a way that he hoped would end by making a poet of him, but it hadn't worked. That was the long and short of it. So he might have just gone on to some unimaginably sordid end if Miriam, after four years: four years? yes, good God, four years and one month and eleven days, had not written home for money, packed up what was left of her belongings, called him a few farewell names, and left. She had been shabby and thin and wild-looking for so long he could not remember ever having seen her any other way, yet all at once her profile in the doorway was unrecognizable to him.

So she went, and she did him a great favor without knowing it. He had fallen into the cowardly habit of thinking their marriage was permanent, no matter how evil it might be, that they loved each other, and so it did not matter what cruelties they committed against each other, and he had developed a real deafness to her words. He was unable, towards the end, either to see her or hear her. He realized this afterward, when remembered phrases and expressions of her eyes and mouth began to eat into his marrow. He was grateful to her. If she had not gone, he might have loitered on, wasting his time trying to write poetry, hanging around dirty picturesque little cafés with a fresh set of clever talkative poverty-stricken young Mexicans who were painting or writing or talking about getting ready to paint or write. His faith had renewed itself; these fellows were pure artists —they would never sell out. They were not bums, either. They worked all the time at something to do with Art. "Sacred Art," he said, "our glasses are empty again."

But try telling anything of the kind to Miriam. Somehow he had never got to that tree he meant to lie down under. If he had, somebody would certainly have come around and collected rent for it, anyhow. He had spent a good deal of time lying under tables at Dinty Moore's or the Black Cat with a gang of Americans like himself who were living a free life and studying the native customs. He was rehearsing, he explained to Miriam, hoping for once she would take a joke, for lying under a tree later on. It didn't go over. She would have died with her boots on before she would have cracked a smile at that. So then . . . He had gone in for a career in the hugest sort of way. It had been easy. He hardly could say now just what his first steps were, but it had been easy. Except for Miriam, he would have been a lousy failure, like those bums at Dinty Moore's, still rolling under the tables, studying the native customs. He had gone in for a career in journalism and he had made a good thing of it. He was a recognized authority on revolutions in twenty-odd Latin-American countries, and his sympathies happened to fall in exactly right with the high-priced magazines of a liberal humanitarian slant which paid him well for telling the world about the oppressed peoples. He could really write, too; if he did say so, he had a prose style of his own. He had made the kind of success you can clip out of newspapers and paste in a book, you can count it and put it in the bank, you can eat and drink and wear it, and you can see it in other people's eyes at tea and dinner parties. Fine, and now what? On the strength of all this he had got married again. Twice, in fact, and divorced twice. That made three times, didn't it? That was plenty. He had spent a good deal of time and energy doing all sorts of things he didn't care for in the least to prove to his first wife, who had been a twenty-three-year-old school-teacher in Minneapolis, Minnesota, that he was not just merely a bum, fit for nothing but lying under a tree—if he had ever been able to locate that ideal tree he had in his mind's eye—writing poetry and enjoying his life.

Now he had done it. He smoothed out the letter he had been turning in his hands and stroked it as if it were a cat. He said, "I've been working up to the climax all this time. You know, good old surprise technique. Now then, get ready."

Miriam had written to him, after these five years, asking him to take her back. And would you believe it, he was going to break down and do that very thing. Her father was dead, she was terribly lonely, she had had time to think everything over, she believed herself to blame for a great many things, she loved him truly and she always had, truly; she regretted, oh, everything, and hoped it was not too late for them to make a happy life together once more. . . . She had read everything she could find of his in print, and she loved all of it. He had that very morning sent by cable the money for her to travel on, and he was going to take her back. She was going to live again in a Mexican house without any conveniences and she was not going to have a modern flat. She was going to take whatever he chose to hand her, and like it. And he wasn't going to marry her again, either. Not he. If she wanted to live with him on these terms, well and good. If not, she could just go back once more to that school of hers in Minneapolis. If she stayed, she would walk a chalk line, all right, one she hadn't drawn for herself. He picked up a cheese knife and drew a long sharp line in the checkered table-cloth. She would, believe him, walk *that*.

The hands of the clock pointed half past two. The journalist swallowed the last of his drink and went on drawing more cross-hatches on the table-cloth with a relaxed hand. His guest wished to say, "Don't forget to invite me to your wedding," but thought better of it. The journalist raised his twitching lids and swung his half-focused eyes upon the shadow opposite and said, "I suppose you think I don't know—"

His guest moved to the chair edge and watched the orchestra folding up for the night. The café was almost empty. The journalist paused, not for an answer, but to give weight to the important statement he was about to make.

"I don't know what's happening, this time," he said, "don't deceive yourself. This time, I know." He seemed to be admonishing himself before a mirror.

THE JILTING OF
GRANNY WEATHERALL

The Jilting of Granny Weatherall

SHE flicked her wrist neatly out of Doctor Harry's pudgy careful fingers and pulled the sheet up to her chin. The brat ought to be in knee breeches. Doctoring around the country with spectacles on his nose! "Get along now, take your schoolbooks and go. There's nothing wrong with me."

Doctor Harry spread a warm paw like a cushion on her forehead where the forked green vein danced and made her eyelids twitch. "Now, now, be a good girl, and we'll have you up in no time."

"That's no way to speak to a woman nearly eighty years old just because she's down. I'd have you respect your elders, young man."

"Well, Missy, excuse me." Doctor Harry patted her cheek. "But I've got to warn you, haven't I? You're a marvel, but you must be careful or you're going to be good and sorry."

"Don't tell me what I'm going to be. I'm on my feet now, morally speaking. It's Cornelia. I had to go to bed to get rid of her."

Her bones felt loose, and floated around in her skin,

and Doctor Harry floated like a balloon around the foot of the bed. He floated and pulled down his waistcoat and swung his glasses on a cord. "Well, stay where you are, it certainly can't hurt you."

"Get along and doctor your sick," said Granny Weatherall. "Leave a well woman alone. I'll call for you when I want you. . . . Where were you forty years ago when I pulled through milk-leg and double pneumonia? You weren't even born. Don't let Cornelia lead you on," she shouted, because Doctor Harry appeared to float up to the ceiling and out. "I pay my own bills, and I don't throw my money away on nonsense!"

She meant to wave good-by, but it was too much trouble. Her eyes closed of themselves, it was like a dark curtain drawn around the bed. The pillow rose and floated under her, pleasant as a hammock in a light wind. She listened to the leaves rustling outside the window. No, somebody was swishing newspapers: no, Cornelia and Doctor Harry were whispering together. She leaped broad awake, thinking they whispered in her ear.

"She was never like this, *never* like this!" "Well, what can we expect?" "Yes, eighty years old. . . ."

Well, and what if she was? She still had ears. It was like Cornelia to whisper around doors. She always kept things secret in such a public way. She was always being tactful and kind. Cornelia was dutiful; that was the trouble with her. Dutiful and good: "So good and dutiful," said Granny, "that I'd like to spank her." She saw herself spanking Cornelia and making a fine job of it

"What'd you say, Mother?"

Granny felt her face tying up in hard knots.

"Can't a body think, I'd like to know?"

"I thought you might want something."

"I do. I want a lot of things. First off, go away and don't whisper."

She lay and drowsed, hoping in her sleep that the children would keep out and let her rest a minute. It had been a long day. Not that she was tired. It was always pleasant to snatch a minute now and then. There was always so much to be done, let me see: tomorrow.

Tomorrow was far away and there was nothing to trouble about. Things were finished somehow when the time came; thank God there was always a little margin over for peace: then a person could spread out the plan of life and tuck in the edges orderly. It was good to have everything clean and folded away, with the hair brushes and tonic bottles sitting straight on the white embroidered linen: the day started without fuss and the pantry shelves laid out with rows of jelly glasses and brown jugs and white stone-china jars with blue whirligigs and words painted on them: coffee, tea, sugar, ginger, cinnamon, allspice: and the bronze clock with the lion on top nicely dusted off. The dust that lion could collect in twenty-four hours! The box in the attic with all those letters tied up, well, she'd have to go through that tomorrow. All those letters—George's letters and John's letters and her letters to them both—lying around for the children to find afterwards made her uneasy. Yes, that would be tomorrow's business. No use to let them know how silly she had been once.

While she was rummaging around she found death in her mind and it felt clammy and unfamiliar. She had spent so much time preparing for death there was no need for bringing it up again. Let it take care of itself now. When she was sixty she had felt very old, finished, and went around making farewell trips to see her children and grandchildren, with a secret in her mind: This is the very last of your mother, children! Then she made her will and came down with a long fever. That was all just a notion like a lot of other things, but it was lucky too, for she had once for all got over the idea of dying for a long time. Now she couldn't be worried. She hoped she had better sense now. Her father had lived to be one hundred and two years old and had drunk a noggin of strong hot toddy on his last birthday. He told the reporters it was his daily habit, and he owed his long life to that. He had made quite a scandal and was very pleased about it. She believed she'd just plague Cornelia a little.

"Cornelia! Cornelia!" No footsteps, but a sudden hand on her cheek. "Bless you, where have you been?"

"Here, mother."

"Well, Cornelia, I want a noggin of hot toddy."

"Are you cold, darling?"

"I'm chilly, Cornelia. Lying in bed stops the circulation. I must have told you that a thousand times."

Well, she could just hear Cornelia telling her husband that Mother was getting a little childish and they'd have to humor her. The thing that most annoyed her was that Cornelia thought she was deaf, dumb, and blind. Little hasty glances and tiny gestures tossed around her and over her head saying, "Don't cross her, let her have her way, she's eighty years old," and she sitting there as if she lived in a thin glass cage. Sometimes Granny almost made up her mind to pack up and move back to her own house where nobody could remind her every minute that she was old. Wait, wait, Cornelia, till your own children whisper behind your back!

In her day she had kept a better house and had got more work done. She wasn't too old yet for Lydia to be driving eighty miles for advice when one of the children jumped the track, and Jimmy still dropped in and talked things over: "Now, Mammy, you've a good busi-

ness head, I want to know what you think of this? . . ."
Old. Cornelia couldn't change the furniture around
without asking. Little things, little things! They had been
so sweet when they were little. Granny wished the old
days were back again with the children young and
everything to be done over. It had been a hard pull, but
not too much for her. When she thought of all the food
she had cooked, and all the clothes she had cut and
sewed, and all the gardens she had made—well, the children showed it. There they were, made out of her, and
they couldn't get away from that. Sometimes she wanted
to see John again and point to them and say, Well, I
didn't do so badly, did I? But that would have to wait.
That was for tomorrow. She used to think of him as a
man, but now all the children were older than their
father, and he would be a child beside her if she saw
him now. It seemed strange and there was something
wrong in the idea. Why, he couldn't possibly recognize
her. She had fenced in a hundred acres once, digging
the post holes herself and clamping the wires with just
a negro boy to help. That changed a woman. John would
be looking for a young woman with the peaked Spanish
comb in her hair and the painted fan. Digging post holes
changed a woman. Riding country roads in the winter
when women had their babies was another thing: sitting
up nights with sick horses and sick negroes and sick

children and hardly ever losing one. John, I hardly ever lost one of them! John would see that in a minute, that would be something he could understand, she wouldn't have to explain anything!

It made her feel like rolling up her sleeves and putting the whole place to rights again. No matter if Cornelia was determined to be everywhere at once, there were a great many things left undone on this place. She would start tomorrow and do them. It was good to be strong enough for everything, even if all you made melted and changed and slipped under your hands, so that by the time you finished you almost forgot what you were working for. What was it I set out to do? she asked herself intently, but she could not remember. A fog rose over the valley, she saw it marching across the creek swallowing the trees and moving up the hill like an army of ghosts. Soon it would be at the near edge of the orchard, and then it was time to go in and light the lamps. Come in, children, don't stay out in the night air.

Lighting the lamps had been beautiful. The children huddled up to her and breathed like little calves waiting at the bars in the twilight. Their eyes followed the match and watched the flame rise and settle in a blue curve, then they moved away from her. The lamp was lit, they didn't have to be scared and hang on to mother any more. Never, never, never more. God, for all my life I thank Thee. Without Thee, my God, I could never have done it. Hail, Mary, full of grace.

I want you to pick all the fruit this year and see that nothing is wasted. There's always someone who can use it. Don't let good things rot for want of using. You waste life when you waste good food. Don't let things get lost. It's bitter to lose things. Now, don't let me get to thinking, not when I am tired and taking a little nap before supper. . . .

The pillow rose about her shoulders and pressed against her heart and the memory was being squeezed out of it: oh, push down the pillow, somebody: it would smother her if she tried to hold it. Such a fresh breeze blowing and such a green day with no threats in it. But he had not come, just the same. What does a woman do when she has put on the white veil and set out the white cake for a man and he doesn't come? She tried to remember. No, I swear he never harmed me but in that. He never harmed me but in that . . . and what if he did? There was the day, the day, but a whirl of dark smoke rose and covered it, crept up and over into the bright field where everything was planted so carefully in orderly rows. That was hell, she knew hell when she saw it. For sixty years she had prayed against remembering him and against losing her soul in the deep pit of hell, and now the two things were mingled in one and the thought of him was a smoky cloud from hell that moved and crept in her head when she had just got rid of Doctor Harry and was trying to rest a minute. Wounded vanity, Ellen, said a sharp voice in the top of her mind. Don't let your wounded vanity get the upper hand of you. Plenty of girls get jilted. You were jilted, weren't you? Then stand up to it. Her eyelids wavered and let in streamers of blue-gray light like tissue paper over her eyes. She must get up and pull the shades down or she'd never sleep. She was in bed again and the shades were not down. How could that happen? Better turn over, hide from the light, sleeping in the light gave you nightmares. "Mother, how do you feel now?" and a stinging wetness on her forehead. But I don't like having my face washed in cold water!

Hapsy? George? Lydia? Jimmy? No, Cornelia, and her features were swollen and full of little puddles. "They're coming, darling, they'll all be here soon." Go wash your face, child, you look funny.

Instead of obeying, Cornelia knelt down and put her head on the pillow. She seemed to be talking but there was no sound. "Well, are you tongue-tied? Whose birthday is it? Are you going to give a party?"

Cornelia's mouth moved urgently in strange shapes. "Don't do that, you bother me, daughter."

"Oh, no, Mother. Oh, no. . . ."

Nonsense. It was strange about children. They disputed your every word. "No what, Cornelia?"

"Here's Doctor Harry."

"I won't see that boy again. He just left five minutes ago."

"That was this morning, Mother. It's night now. Here's the nurse."

"This is Doctor Harry, Mrs. Weatherall. I never saw you look so young and happy!"

"Ah, I'll never be young again—but I'd be happy if they'd let me lie in peace and get rested."

She thought she spoke up loudly, but no one answered. A warm weight on her forehead, a warm bracelet on her wrist, and a breeze went on whispering, trying to tell her something. A shuffle of leaves in the everlasting hand of God, He blew on them and they danced and rattled. "Mother, don't mind, we're going to give you a little hypodermic." "Look here, daughter, how do ants get in this bed? I saw sugar ants yesterday." Did you send for Hapsy too?

It was Hapsy she really wanted. She had to go a long way back through a great many rooms to find Hapsy standing with a baby on her arm. She seemed to herself to be Hapsy also, and the baby on Hapsy's arm was Hapsy and himself and herself, all at once, and there was no surprise in the meeting. Then Hapsy melted from within and turned flimsy as gray gauze and the baby was a gauzy shadow, and Hapsy came up close and said, "I thought you'd never come," and looked at her very searchingly and said, "You haven't changed a bit!" They leaned forward to kiss, when Cornelia began whispering from a long way off, "Oh, is there anything you want to tell me? Is there anything I can do for you?"

Yes, she had changed her mind after sixty years and she would like to see George. I want you to find George. Find him and be sure to tell him I forgot him. I want him to know I had my husband just the same and my children and my house like any other woman. A good house too and a good husband that I loved and fine children out of him. Better than I hoped for even. Tell him I was given back everything he took away and more. Oh, no, oh, God, no, there was something else besides the house and the man and the children. Oh, surely they were not all? What was it? Something not given back. . . . Her breath crowded down under her ribs and grew into a monstrous frightening shape with cutting edges; it bored up into her head, and the agony was unbelievable: Yes, John, get the Doctor now, no more talk, my time has come.

When this one was born it should be the last. The last. It should have been born first, for it was the one she had truly wanted. Everything came in good time. Nothing left out, left over. She was strong, in three days she would be as well as ever. Better. A woman needed milk in her to have her full health.

"Mother, do you hear me?"

"I've been telling you—"

"Mother, Father Connolly's here."

"I went to Holy Communion only last week. Tell him I'm not so sinful as all that."

"Father just wants to speak to you."

He could speak as much as he pleased. It was like him to drop in and inquire about her soul as if it were a teething baby, and then stay on for a cup of tea and a round of cards and gossip. He always had a funny story of some sort, usually about an Irishman who made his little mistakes and confessed them, and the point lay in some absurd thing he would blurt out in the confessional showing his struggles between native piety and original sin. Granny felt easy about her soul. Cornelia, where are your manners? Give Father Connolly a chair. She had her secret comfortable understanding with a few favorite saints who cleared a straight road to God for her. All as surely signed and sealed as the papers for the new Forty Acres. Forever . . . heirs and assigns forever. Since the day the wedding cake was not cut, but thrown out and wasted. The whole bottom dropped out of the world, and there she was blind and sweating with nothing under her feet and the walls falling away. His hand had caught her under the breast, she had not fallen, there was the freshly polished floor with the green rug on it, just as before. He had cursed like a sailor's parrot and said, "I'll kill him for you." Don't lay a hand on him, for my sake leave something to God. "Now, Ellen, you must believe what I tell you. . . ."

So there was nothing, nothing to worry about any more, except sometimes in the night one of the children screamed in a nightmare, and they both hustled out shaking and hunting for the matches and calling, "There, wait a minute, here we are!" John, get the doctor now, Hapsy's time has come. But there was Hapsy standing by the bed in a white cap. "Cornelia, tell Hapsy to take off her cap. I can't see her plain."

Her eyes opened very wide and the room stood out like a picture she had seen somewhere. Dark colors with the shadows rising towards the ceiling in long angles. The tall black dresser gleamed with nothing on it but John's picture, enlarged from a little one, with John's eyes very black when they should have been blue. You never saw him, so how do you know how he looked? But the man insisted the copy was perfect, it was very rich and handsome. For a picture, yes, but it's not my husband. The table by the bed had a linen cover and a candle and a crucifix. The light was blue from Cornelia's silk lampshades. No sort of light at all, just frippery. You had to live forty years with kerosene lamps to appreciate honest electricity. She felt very strong and she saw Doctor Harry with a rosy nimbus around him.

"You look like a saint, Doctor Harry, and I vow that's as near as you'll ever come to it."

"She's saying something."

'I heard you, Cornelia. What's all this carrying-on?"

"Father Connolly's saying—"

Cornelia's voice staggered and bumped like a cart in a bad road. It rounded corners and turned back again and arrived nowhere. Granny stepped up in the cart very lightly and reached for the reins, but a man sat beside her and she knew him by his hands, driving the cart. She did not look in his face, for she knew without seeing, but looked instead down the road where the trees leaned over and bowed to each other and a thousand birds were singing a Mass. She felt like singing too, but she put her hand in the bosom of her dress and pulled out a rosary, and Father Connolly murmured Latin in a very solemn voice and tickled her feet. My God, will you stop that nonsense? I'm a married woman. What if he did run away and leave me to face the priest by myself? I found another a whole world better. I wouldn't have exchanged my husband for anybody ex-

cept St. Michael himself, and you may tell him that for
me with a thank you in the bargain.

Light flashed on her closed eyelids, and a deep roaring
shook her. Cornelia, is that lightning? I hear thunder.
There's going to be a storm. Close all the windows. Call
the children in. . . . "Mother, here we are, all of us."
"Is that you, Hapsy?" "Oh, no, I'm Lydia. We drove
as fast as we could." Their faces drifted above her,
drifted away. The rosary fell out of her hands and Lydia
put it back. Jimmy tried to help, their hands fumbled
together, and Granny closed two fingers around Jimmy's
thumb. Beads wouldn't do, it must be something alive.
She was so amazed her thoughts ran round and round.
So, my dear Lord, this is my death and I wasn't even
thinking about it. My children have come to see me die.
But I can't, it's not time. Oh, I always hated surprises.
I wanted to give Cornelia the amethyst set—Cornelia,
you're to have the amethyst set, but Hapsy's to wear
it when she wants, and, Doctor Harry, do shut up. Nobody sent for you. Oh, my dear Lord, do wait a minute. I meant to do something about the Forty Acres,
Jimmy doesn't need it and Lydia will later on, with that
worthless husband of hers. I meant to finish the altar
cloth and send six bottles of wine to Sister Borgia for
her dyspepsia. I want to send six bottles of wine to Sister
Borgia, Father Connolly, now don't let me forget.

Cornelia's voice made short turns and tilted over and crashed. "Oh, Mother, oh, Mother, oh, Mother. . . ."

"I'm not going, Cornelia. I'm taken by surprise. I can't go."

You'll see Hapsy again. What about her? "I thought you'd never come." Granny made a long journey outward, looking for Hapsy. What if I don't find her? What then? Her heart sank down and down, there was no bottom to death, she couldn't come to the end of it. The blue light from Cornelia's lampshade drew into a tiny point in the center of her brain, it flickered and winked like an eye, quietly it fluttered and dwindled. Granny lay curled down within herself, amazed and watchful, staring at the point of light that was herself; her body was now only a deeper mass of shadow in an endless darkness and this darkness would curl around the light and swallow it up. God, give a sign!

For the second time there was no sign. Again no bridegroom and the priest in the house. She could not remember any other sorrow because this grief wiped them all away. Oh, no, there's nothing more cruel than this—I'll never forgive it. She stretched herself with a deep breath and blew out the light.

FLOWERING JUDAS

Flowering Judas

BRAGGIONI sits heaped upon the edge of a straight-backed chair much too small for him, and sings to Laura in a furry, mournful voice. Laura has begun to find reasons for avoiding her own house until the latest possible moment, for Braggioni is there almost every night. No matter how late she is, he will be sitting there with a surly, waiting expression, pulling at his kinky yellow hair, thumbing the strings of his guitar, snarling a tune under his breath. Lupe the Indian maid meets Laura at the door, and says with a flicker of a glance towards the upper room, "He waits."

Laura wishes to lie down, she is tired of her hairpins and the feel of her long tight sleeves, but she says to him, "Have you a new song for me this evening?" If he says yes, she asks him to sing it. If he says no, she remembers his favorite one, and asks him to sing it again. Lupe brings her a cup of chocolate and a plate of rice, and Laura eats at the small table under the lamp, first inviting Braggioni, whose answer is always the same: "I have eaten, and besides, chocolate thickens the voice."

Laura says, "Sing, then," and Braggioni heaves himself into song. He scratches the guitar familiarly as though it were a pet animal, and sings passionately off key, taking the high notes in a prolonged painful squeal. Laura, who haunts the markets listening to the ballad singers, and stops every day to hear the blind boy playing his reed-flute in Sixteenth of September Street, listens to Braggioni with pitiless courtesy, because she dares not smile at his miserable performance. Nobody dares to smile at him. Braggioni is cruel to everyone, with a kind of specialized insolence, but he is so vain of his talents, and so sensitive to slights, it would require a cruelty and vanity greater than his own to lay a finger on the vast cureless wound of his self-esteem. It would require courage, too, for it is dangerous to offend him, and nobody has this courage.

Braggioni loves himself with such tenderness and amplitude and eternal charity that his followers—for he is a leader of men, a skilled revolutionist, and his skin has been punctured in honorable warfare—warm themselves in the reflected glow, and say to each other: "He has a real nobility, a love of humanity raised above mere personal affections." The excess of this self-love has flowed out, inconveniently for her, over Laura, who, with so many others, owes her comfortable situation and her salary to him. When he is in a very good humor, he tells her, "I am tempted to forgive you for being a

gringa. Gringita!" and Laura, burning, imagines
leaning forward suddenly, and with a sound back-hand
slap wiping the suety smile from his face. If he notices
her eyes at these moments he gives no sign.

She knows what Braggioni would offer her, and she
must resist tenaciously without appearing to resist, and
if she could avoid it she would not admit even to herself
the slow drift of his intention. During these long evenings which have spoiled a long month for her, she sits
in her deep chair with an open book on her knees, resting her eyes on the consoling rigidity of the printed page
when the sight and sound of Braggioni singing threaten
to identify themselves with all her remembered afflictions and to add their weight to her uneasy premonitions
of the future. The gluttonous bulk of Braggioni has become a symbol of her many disillusions, for a revolutionist should be lean, animated by heroic faith, a vessel
of abstract virtues. This is nonsense, she knows it now
and is ashamed of it. Revolution must have leaders, and
leadership is a career for energetic men. She is, her comrades tell her, full of romantic error, for what she defines
as cynicism in them is merely "a developed sense of
reality." She is almost too willing to say, "I am wrong,
I suppose I don't really understand the principles," and
afterward she makes a secret truce with herself, determined not to surrender her will to such expedient

logic. But she cannot help feeling that she has been betrayed irreparably by the disunion between her way of living and her feeling of what life should be, and at times she is almost contented to rest in this sense of grievance as a private store of consolation. Sometimes she wishes to run away, but she stays. Now she longs to fly out of this room, down the narrow stairs, and into the street where the houses lean together like conspirators under a single mottled lamp, and leave Braggioni singing to himself.

Instead she looks at Braggioni, frankly and clearly, like a good child who understands the rules of behavior. Her knees cling together under sound blue serge, and her round white collar is not purposely nun-like. She wears the uniform of an idea, and has renounced vanities. She was born Roman Catholic, and in spite of her fear of being seen by someone who might make a scandal of it, she slips now and again into some crumbling little church, kneels on the chilly stone, and says a Hail Mary on the gold rosary she bought in Tehuantepec. It is no good and she ends by examining the altar with its tinsel flowers and ragged brocades, and feels tender about the battered doll-shape of some male saint whose white, lace-trimmed drawers hang limply around his ankles below the hieratic dignity of his velvet robe. She has encased herself in a set of principles derived from her early training, leaving no detail of gesture or of personal taste untouched, and for this reason she will not wear lace made on machines. This is her private heresy, for in her special group the machine is sacred, and will be the salvation of the workers. She loves fine lace, and there is a tiny edge of fluted cobweb on this collar, which is one of twenty precisely alike, folded in blue tissue paper in the upper drawer of her clothes chest.

Braggioni catches her glance solidly as if he had been waiting for it, leans forward, balancing his paunch between his spread knees, and sings with tremendous emphasis, weighing his words. He has, the song relates, no father and no mother, nor even a friend to console him; lonely as a wave of the sea he comes and goes, lonely as a wave. His mouth opens round and yearns sideways, his balloon cheeks grow oily with the labor of song. He bulges marvelously in his expensive garments. Over his lavender collar, crushed upon a purple necktie, held by a diamond hoop: over his ammunition belt of tooled leather worked in silver, buckled cruelly around his gasping middle: over the tops of his glossy yellow shoes Braggioni swells with ominous ripeness, his mauve silk hose stretched taut, his ankles bound with the stout leather thongs of his shoes.

When he stretches his eyelids at Laura she notes again that his eyes are the true tawny yellow cat's eyes. He is rich, not in money, he tells her, but in power, and this power brings with it the blameless ownership of things, and the right to indulge his love of small luxuries. "I have a taste for the elegant refinements," he said once, flourishing a yellow silk handkerchief before her nose. "Smell that? It is Jockey Club, imported from New York." Nonetheless he is wounded by life. He will say so presently. "It is true everything turns to dust in the hand, to gall on the tongue." He sighs and his leather belt creaks like a saddle girth. "I am disappointed in everything as it comes. Everything." He shakes his head. "You, poor thing, you will be disappointed too. You are born for it. We are more alike than you realize in some things. Wait and see. Some day you will remember what I have told you, you will know that Braggioni was your friend."

Laura feels a slow chill, a purely physical sense of danger, a warning in her blood that violence, mutilation, a shocking death, wait for her with lessening patience. She has translated this fear into something homely, immediate, and sometimes hesitates before crossing the street. "My personal fate is nothing, except as the testimony of a mental attitude," she reminds herself, quoting from some forgotten philosophic primer, and is sensible enough to add, "Anyhow, I shall not be killed by an automobile if I can help it."

"It may be true I am as corrupt, in another way, as Braggioni," she thinks in spite of herself, "as callous, as incomplete," and if this is so, any kind of death seems preferable. Still she sits quietly, she does not run. Where could she go? Uninvited she has promised herself to this place; she can no longer imagine herself as living in another country, and there is no pleasure in remembering her life before she came here.

Precisely what is the nature of this devotion, its true motives, and what are its obligations? Laura cannot say. She spends part of her days in Xochimilco, near by, teaching Indian children to say in English, "The cat is on the mat." When she appears in the classroom they crowd about her with smiles on their wise, innocent, clay-colored faces, crying, "Good morning, my titcher!" in immaculate voices, and they make of her desk a fresh garden of flowers every day.

During her leisure she goes to union meetings and listens to busy important voices quarreling over tactics, methods, internal politics. She visits the prisoners of her own political faith in their cells, where they entertain themselves with counting cockroaches, repenting of their indiscretions, composing their memoirs, writing out manifestoes and plans for their comrades who are still walking about free, hands in pockets, sniffing fresh air. Laura brings them food and cigarettes and a little money, and she brings messages disguised in equivocal phrases from the men outside who dare not set foot in the prison for fear of disappearing into the cells kept empty for them. If the prisoners confuse night and day, and complain, "Dear little Laura, time doesn't pass in this infernal hole, and I won't know when it is time to sleep unless I have a reminder," she brings them their favorite narcotics, and says in a tone that does not wound them with pity, "Tonight will really be night for you," and though her Spanish amuses them, they find her comforting, useful. If they lose patience and all faith, and curse the slowness of their friends in coming to their rescue with money and influence, they trust her not to repeat everything, and if she inquires, "Where do you think we can find money, or influence?" they are certain to answer, "Well, there is Braggioni, why doesn't he do something?"

She smuggles letters from headquarters to men hiding from firing squads in back streets in mildewed houses, where they sit in tumbled beds and talk bitterly as if all Mexico were at their heels, when Laura knows positively they might appear at the band concert in the Alameda on Sunday morning, and no one would notice them. But Braggioni says, "Let them sweat a little. The next time they may be careful. It is very restful to have them out of the way for a while." She is not afraid to

knock on any door in any street after midnight, and
enter in the darkness, and say to one of these men who
is really in danger: "They will be looking for you—
seriously—tomorrow morning after six. Here is some
money from Vicente. Go to Vera Cruz and wait."

She borrows money from the Roumanian agitator to
give to his bitter enemy the Polish agitator. The favor
of Braggioni is their disputed territory, and Braggioni
holds the balance nicely, for he can use them both. The
Polish agitator talks love to her over café tables, hoping
to exploit what he believes is her secret sentimental pref-
erence for him, and he gives her misinformation which
he begs her to repeat as the solemn truth to certain persons. The Roumanian is more adroit. He is generous
with his money in all good causes, and lies to her with
an air of ingenuous candor, as if he were her good friend
and confidant. She never repeats anything they may say.
Braggioni never asks questions. He has other ways to
discover all that he wishes to know about them.

Nobody touches her, but all praise her gray eyes, and
the soft, round under lip which promises gayety, yet
is always grave, nearly always firmly closed: and they
cannot understand why she is in Mexico. She walks
back and forth on her errands, with puzzled eyebrows,
carrying her little folder of drawings and music and
school papers. No dancer dances more beautifully than

Laura walks, and she inspires some amusing, unexpected ardors, which cause little gossip, because nothing comes of them. A young captain who had been a soldier in Zapata's army attempted, during a horseback ride near Cuernavaca, to express his desire for her with the noble simplicity befitting a rude folk-hero: but gently, because he was gentle. This gentleness was his defeat, for when he alighted, and removed her foot from the stirrup, and essayed to draw her down into his arms, her horse, ordinarily a tame one, shied fiercely, reared and plunged away. The young hero's horse careered blindly after his stable-mate, and the hero did not return to the hotel until rather late that evening. At breakfast he came to her table in full charro dress, gray buckskin jacket and trousers with strings of silver buttons down the leg, and he was in a humorous, careless mood. "May I sit with you?" and "You are a wonderful rider. I was terrified that you might be thrown and dragged. I should never have forgiven myself. But I cannot admire you enough for your riding!"

"I learned to ride in Arizona," said Laura.

"If you will ride with me again this morning, I promise you a horse that will not shy with you," he said. But Laura remembered that she must return to Mexico City at noon.

Next morning the children made a celebration and

spent their playtime writing on the blackboard, "We lov ar ticher," and with tinted chalks they drew wreaths of flowers around the words. The young hero wrote her a letter: "I am a very foolish, wasteful, impulsive man. I should have first said I love you, and then you would not have run away. But you shall see me again." Laura thought, "I must send him a box of colored crayons," but she was trying to forgive herself for having spurred her horse at the wrong moment.

A brown, shock-haired youth came and stood in her patio one night and sang like a lost soul for two hours, but Laura could think of nothing to do about it. The moonlight spread a wash of gauzy silver over the clear spaces of the garden, and the shadows were cobalt blue. The scarlet blossoms of the Judas tree were dull purple, and the names of the colors repeated themselves automatically in her mind, while she watched not the boy, but his shadow, fallen like a dark garment across the fountain rim, trailing in the water. Lupe came silently and whispered expert counsel in her ear: "If you will throw him one little flower, he will sing another song or two and go away." Laura threw the flower, and he sang a last song and went away with the flower tucked in the band of his hat. Lupe said, "He is one of the organizers of the Typographers Union, and before that he sold corridos in the Merced market, and before that,

149

he came from Guanajuato, where I was born. I would not trust any man, but I trust least those from Guanajuato."

She did not tell Laura that he would be back again the next night, and the next, nor that he would follow her at a certain fixed distance around the Merced market, through the Zócolo, up Francisco I. Madero Avenue, and so along the Paseo de la Reforma to Chapultepec Park, and into the Philosopher's Footpath, still with that flower withering in his hat, and an indivisible attention in his eyes.

Now Laura is accustomed to him, it means nothing except that he is nineteen years old and is observing a convention with all propriety, as though it were founded on a law of nature, which in the end it might well prove to be. He is beginning to write poems which he prints on a wooden press, and he leaves them stuck like handbills in her door. She is pleasantly disturbed by the abstract, unhurried watchfulness of his black eyes which will in time turn easily towards another object. She tells herself that throwing the flower was a mistake, for she is twenty-two years old and knows better; but she refuses to regret it, and persuades herself that her negation of all external events as they occur is a sign that she is gradually perfecting herself in the stoicism she strives to cultivate against that disaster she fears, though she cannot name it.

She is not at home in the world. Every day she teaches children who remain strangers to her, though she loves their tender round hands and their charming op-portunist savagery. She knocks at unfamiliar doors not knowing whether a friend or a stranger shall answer, and even if a known face emerges from the sour gloom of that unknown interior, still it is the face of a stranger. No matter what this stranger says to her, nor what her message to him, the very cells of her flesh reject knowl-edge and kinship in one monotonous word. No. No. No. She draws her strength from this one holy talismanic word which does not suffer her to be led into evil. Deny-ing everything, she may walk anywhere in safety, she looks at everything without amazement.

No, repeats this firm unchanging voice of her blood; and she looks at Braggioni without amazement. He is a great man, he wishes to impress this simple girl who covers her great round breasts with thick dark cloth, and who hides long, invaluably beautiful legs under a heavy skirt. She is almost thin except for the incomprehensible fullness of her breasts, like a nursing mother's, and Brag-gioni, who considers himself a judge of women, specu-lates again on the puzzle of her notorious virginity, and takes the liberty of speech which she permits without a sign of modesty, indeed, without any sort of sign, which is disconcerting.

"You think you are so cold, *gringita!* Wait and see. You will surprise yourself some day! May I be there to advise you!" He stretches his eyelids at her, and his ill-humored cat's eyes waver in a separate glance for the two points of light marking the opposite ends of a smoothly drawn path between the swollen curve of her breasts. He is not put off by that blue serge, nor by her resolutely fixed gaze. There is all the time in the world. His cheeks are bellying with the wind of song. "O girl with the dark eyes," he sings, and reconsiders. "But yours are not dark. I can change all that. O girl with the green eyes, you have stolen my heart away!" then his mind wanders to the song, and Laura feels the weight of his attention being shifted elsewhere. Singing thus, he seems harmless, he is quite harmless, there is nothing to do but sit patiently and say "No," when the moment comes. She draws a full breath, and her mind wanders also, but not far. She dares not wander too far.

Not for nothing has Braggioni taken pains to be a good revolutionist and a professional lover of humanity. He will never die of it. He has the malice, the cleverness, the wickedness, the sharpness of wit, the hardness of heart, stipulated for loving the world profitably. *He will never die of it.* He will live to see himself kicked out from his feeding trough by other hungry world-saviors. Traditionally he must sing in spite of his life which drives him to bloodshed, he tells Laura, for his father was a Tuscany peasant who drifted to Yucatan and married a Maya woman: a woman of race, an aristocrat. They gave him the love and knowledge of music, thus: and under the rip of his thumbnail, the strings of the instrument complain like exposed nerves.

Once he was called Delgadito by all the girls and married women who ran after him; he was so scrawny all his bones showed under his thin cotton clothing, and he could squeeze his emptiness to the very backbone with his two hands. He was a poet and the revolution was only a dream then; too many women loved him and sapped away his youth, and he could never find enough to eat anywhere, anywhere! Now he is a leader of men, crafty men who whisper in his ear, hungry men who wait for hours outside his office for a word with him, emaciated men with wild faces who waylay him at the street gate with a timid, "Comrade, let me tell you . . ." and they blow the foul breath from their empty stomachs in his face.

He is always sympathetic. He gives them handfuls of small coins from his own pocket, he promises them work, there will be demonstrations, they must join the unions and attend the meetings, above all they must be on the watch for spies. They are closer to him than his own brothers, without them he can do nothing—until tomorrow, comrade!

Until tomorrow. "They are stupid, they are lazy, they are treacherous, they would cut my throat for nothing," he says to Laura. He has good food and abundant drink, he hires an automobile and drives in the Paseo on Sunday morning, and enjoys plenty of sleep in a soft bed beside a wife who dares not disturb him; and he sits pampering his bones in easy billows of fat, singing to Laura, who knows and thinks these things about him. When he was fifteen, he tried to drown himself because he loved a girl, his first love, and she laughed at him. "A thousand women have paid for that," and his tight little mouth turns down at the corners. Now he perfumes his hair with Jockey Club, and confides to Laura: "One woman is really as good as another for me, in the dark. I prefer them all."

His wife organizes unions among the girls in the cigarette factories, and walks in picket lines, and even speaks at meetings in the evening. But she cannot be brought to acknowledge the benefits of true liberty. "I tell her I must have my freedom, net. She does not understand my point of view." Laura has heard this many times. Braggioni scratches the guitar and meditates. "She is an instinctively virtuous woman, pure gold, no doubt of that. If she were not, I should lock her up, and she knows it."

His wife, who works so hard for the good of the factory girls, employs part of her leisure lying on the floor weeping because there are so many women in the world, and only one husband for her, and she never knows where nor when to look for him. He told her: "Unless you can learn to cry when I am not here, I must go away for good." That day he went away and took a room at the Hotel Madrid.

It is this month of separation for the sake of higher principles that has been spoiled not only for Mrs. Braggioni, whose sense of reality is beyond criticism, but for Laura, who feels herself bogged in a nightmare. Tonight Laura envies Mrs. Braggioni, who is alone, and free to weep as much as she pleases about a concrete wrong. Laura has just come from a visit to the prison, and she is waiting for tomorrow with a bitter anxiety as if tomorrow may not come, but time may be caught immovably in this hour, with herself transfixed, Braggioni singing on forever, and Eugenio's body not yet discovered by the guard.

Braggioni says: "Are you going to sleep?" Almost before she can shake her head, he begins telling her about the May-day disturbances coming on in Morelia, for the Catholics hold a festival in honor of the Blessed Virgin, and the Socialists celebrate their martyrs on that day. "There will be two independent processions, starting from either end of town, and they will march until they meet, and the rest depends . . ." He asks her to oil and load his pistols. Standing up, he unbuckles his ammunition belt, and spreads it laden across her knees. Laura sits with the shells slipping through the cleaning cloth dipped in oil, and he says again he cannot understand why she works so hard for the revolutionary idea unless she loves some man who is in it. "Are you not in love with someone?" "No," says Laura. "And no one is in love with you?" "No." "Then it is your own fault. No woman need go begging. Why, what is the matter with you? The legless beggar woman in the Alameda has a perfectly faithful lover. Did you know that?"

Laura peers down the pistol barrel and says nothing, but a long, slow faintness rises and subsides in her; Braggioni curves his swollen fingers around the throat of the guitar and softly smothers the music out of it, and when she hears him again he seems to have forgotten her, and is speaking in the hypnotic voice he uses when talking in small rooms to a listening, close-gathered crowd. Some day this world, now seemingly so composed and eternal, to the edges of every sea shall be merely a tangle of gaping trenches, of crashing walls and broken bodies. Everything must be torn from its accustomed place where it has rotted for centuries, hurled skyward and distributed, cast down again clean as rain, without separate identity. Nothing shall survive that the stiffened hands of poverty have created for the rich and no one shall be left alive except the elect spirits destined to procreate a new world cleansed of cruelty and injustice, ruled by benevolent anarchy: "Pistols are good, I love them, cannon are even better, but in the end I pin my faith to good dynamite," he concludes, and strokes the pistol lying in her hands. "Once I dreamed of destroying this city, in case it offered resistance to General Ortíz, but it fell into his hands like an overripe pear."

He is made restless by his own words, rises and stands waiting. Laura holds up the belt to him: "Put that on, and go kill somebody in Morelia, and you will be happier," she says softly. The presence of death in the room makes her bold. "Today, I found Eugenio going into a stupor. He refused to allow me to call the prison doctor. He had taken all the tablets I brought him yesterday. He said he took them because he was bored."

"He is a fool, and his death is his own business," says Braggioni, fastening his belt carefully.

"I told him if he had waited only a little while longer, you would have got him set free," says Laura. "He said he did not want to wait."

"He is a fool and we are well rid of him," says Braggioni, reaching for his hat.

He goes away. Laura knows his mood has changed, she will not see him any more for a while. He will send word when he needs her to go on errands into strange streets, to speak to the strange faces that will appear, like clay masks with the power of human speech, to mutter their thanks to Braggioni for his help. Now she is free, and she thinks, I must run while there is time. But she does not go.

Braggioni enters his own house where for a month his wife has spent many hours every night weeping and tangling her hair upon her pillow. She is weeping now, and she weeps more at the sight of him, the cause of all her sorrows. He looks about the room. Nothing is changed, the smells are good and familiar, he is well acquainted with the woman who comes toward him with no reproach except grief on her face. He says to her tenderly: "You are so good, please don't cry any more, you dear good creature." She says, "Are you tired, my angel? Sit here and I will wash your feet." She brings a bowl of water, and kneeling, unlaces his shoes, and when from her knees she raises her sad eyes under her blackened lids, he is sorry for everything, and bursts into tears. "Ah, yes, I am hungry, I am tired, let us eat something together," he says, between sobs. His wife leans her head on his arm and says, "Forgive me!" and this time he is refreshed by the solemn, endless rain of her tears.

Laura takes off her serge dress and puts on a white linen nightgown and goes to bed. She turns her head a little to one side, and lying still, reminds herself that it is time to sleep. Numbers tick in her brain like little clocks, soundless doors close of themselves around her. If you would sleep, you must not remember anything, the children will say tomorrow, good morning, my teacher, the poor prisoners who come every day bringing flowers to their jailor. 1-2-3-4-5—it is monstrous to confuse love with revolution, night with day, life with death—ah, Eugenio!

The tolling of the midnight bell is a signal, but what does it mean? Get up, Laura, and follow me: come out of your sleep, out of your bed, out of this strange house. What are you doing in this house? Without a word, without fear she rose and reached for Eugenio's hand, but he eluded her with a sharp, sly smile and drifted away. This is not all, you shall see—Murderer, he said, follow me, I will show you a new country, but it is far away and we must hurry. No, said Laura, not unless you take my hand, no; and she clung first to the stair rail, and then to the topmost branch of the Judas tree that bent down slowly and set her upon the earth, and then to the rocky ledge of a cliff, and then to the jagged wave of a sea that was not water but a desert of crumbling stone. Where are you taking me, she asked in wonder but without fear. To death, and it is a long way off, and we must hurry, said Eugenio. No, said Laura, not unless you take my hand. Then eat these flowers, poor prisoner, said Eugenio in a voice of pity, take and eat: and from the Judas tree he stripped the warm bleeding flowers, and held them to her lips. She saw that his hand was fleshless, a cluster of small white petrified branches, and his eye sockets were without light, but she ate the flowers greedily for they satisfied both hunger and thirst. Murderer! said Eugenio, and Cannibal! This is my body and my blood. Laura cried No! and at the sound of her own voice, she awoke trembling, and was afraid to sleep again.

THE CRACKED
LOOKING-GLASS

The Cracked Looking-Glass

DENNIS heard Rosaleen talking in the kitchen and a man's voice answering. He sat with his hands dangling over his knees, and thought for the hundredth time that sometimes Rosaleen's voice was company to him, and other days he wished all day long she didn't have so much to say about everything. More and more the years put a quietus on a man; there was no earthly sense in saying the same things over and over. Even thinking the same thoughts grew tiresome after a while. But Rosaleen was full of talk as ever. If not to him, to whatever pass-er-by stopped for a minute, and if nobody stopped, she talked to the cats and to herself. If Dennis came near she merely raised her voice and went on with whatever she was saying, so it was nothing for her to shout suddenly, "Come out of that, now—how often have I told ye to keep off the table?" and the cats would scatter in all directions with guilty faces. "It's enough to make a man lep out of his shoes," Dennis would complain. "It's not meant for you, darlin'," Rosaleen would say, as if that cured everything, and if he didn't go away at once, she would start some kind of story. But today she kept shooing him out of the place and hadn't a kind word in her mouth, and Dennis in exile felt that everything and everybody was welcome in the place but himself. For the twentieth time he approached on tiptoe and listened at the parlor keyhole.

Rosaleen was saying: "Maybe his front legs might look a little stuffed for a living cat, but in the picture it's no great matter. I said to Kevin, 'You'll never paint that cat alive,' but Kevin did it, with house paint mixed in a saucer, and a small brush the way he could put in all them fine lines. His legs look like that because I wanted him pictured on the table, but it wasn't so, he was on my lap the whole time. He was a wonder after the mice, a born hunter bringing them in from morning till night—"

Dennis sat on the sofa in the parlor and thought: "There it is. There she goes telling it again." He wondered who the man was, a strange voice, but a loud and ready gabbler as if maybe he was trying to sell something. "It's a fine painting, Miz O'Toole," he said, "and who did you say the artist was?"

"A lad named Kevin, like my own brother he was, who went away to make his fortune," answered Rosaleen. "A house painter by trade."

"The spittin' image of a cat!" roared the voice.

"It is so," said Rosaleen. "The Billy-cat to the life.

The Nelly-cat here is own sister to him, and the Jimmy-cat and the Annie-cat and the Mickey-cat is nephews and nieces, and there's a great family look between all of them. It was the strangest thing happened to the Billy-cat, Mr. Pendleton. He sometimes didn't come in for his supper till after dark, he was so taken up with the hunting, and then one night he didn't come at all, nor the next day neither, nor the next, and me with him on my mind so I didn't get a wink of sleep. Then at midnight on the third night I did go to sleep, and the Billy-cat came into my room and lep upon my pillow and said: 'Up beyond the north field there's a maple tree with a great scar where the branch was taken away by the storm, and near to it is a flat stone, and there you'll find me. I was caught in a trap,' he says; 'wasn't set for me,' he says, 'but it got me all the same. And now be easy in your mind about me,' he says, 'for it's all over.' Then he went away, giving me a look over his shoulder like a human creature, and I woke up Dennis and told him. Surely as we live, Mr. Pendleton, it was all true. So Dennis went beyond the north field and brought him home and we buried him in the garden and cried over him." Her voice broke and lowered and Dennis shuddered for fear she was going to shed tears before this stranger.

"For God's *sake*, Miz O'Toole," said the loudmouthed man, "you can't get around that now, can you? Why, that's the most remarkable thing I ever heard!"

Dennis rose, creaking a little, and hobbled around to the east side of the house in time to see a round man with a flabby red face climbing into a rusty old car with a sign painted on the door. "Always something, now," he commented, putting his head in at the kitchen door. "Always telling a tall tale!"

"Well," said Rosaleen, without the least shame, "he wanted a story so I gave him a good one. That's the Irish in me."

"Always making a thing more than it is," said Dennis. "That's the way it goes."

Rosaleen turned a little edgy. "Out with ye!" she cried, and the cats never budged a whisker. "The kitchen's no place for a man! How often must I tell ye?"

"Well, hand me my hat, will you?" said Dennis, for his hat hung on a nail over the calendar and had hung there within easy reach ever since they had lived in the farmhouse. A few minutes later he wanted his pipe, lying on the lamp shelf where he always kept it. Next he had to have his barn boots at once, though he hadn't seen them for a month. At last he thought of something to say, and opened the door a few inches.

"Wherever have I been sitting unmolested for the past ten years?" he asked, looking at his easy chair with the pillow freshly plumped, sideways to the big table. "And today it's no place for me?"

"If ye grumble ye'll be sorry," said Rosaleen gayly, "and now clear out before I hurl something at ye!"

Dennis put his hat on the parlor table and his boots under the sofa, and sat on the front steps and lit his pipe. It would soon be cold weather, and he wished he had his old leather jacket off the hook on the kitchen door. Whatever was Rosaleen up to now? He decided that Rosaleen was always doing the Irish a great wrong by putting her own faults off on them. To be Irish, he felt, was to be like him, a sober, practical, thinking man, a lover of truth. Rosaleen couldn't see it at all. "It's just your head is like a stone!" she said to him once, pretending she was joking, but she meant it. She had never appreciated him, that was it. And neither had his first wife. Whatever he gave them, they always wanted something else. When he was young and poor his first wife wanted money. And when he was a steady man with money in the bank, his second wife wanted a young man full of life. "They're all born ingrates one way or another," he decided, and felt better at once, as if at last he had something solid to stand on. In September a man could get his death sitting on the steps like this, and little she cared! He clacked his teeth together and felt how they didn't fit any more, and his feet and hands seemed tied on him with strings.

All the while Rosaleen didn't look to be a year older. She might almost be doing it to spite him, except that she wasn't the spiteful kind. He'd be bound to say that for her. But she couldn't forget that her girlhood had been a great triumph in Ireland, and she was forever telling him tales about it, and telling them again. This youth of hers was clearer in his mind than his own. He couldn't remember one thing over another that had happened to him. His past lay like a great lump within him; there it was, he knew it all at once, when he thought of it, like a chest a man has packed away, knowing all that is in it without troubling to name or count the objects. All in a lump it had not been an easy life being named Dennis O'Toole in Bristol, England, where he was brought up and worked sooner than he was able at the first jobs he could find. And his English wife had never forgiven him for pulling her up by the roots and bringing her to New York, where his brothers and sisters were, and a better job. All the long years he had been first a waiter and then head waiter in a New York hotel had telescoped in his mind, somehow. It wasn't the best of hotels, to be sure, but still he was head waiter and there was good money in it, enough to buy this farm in Connecticut and have a little steady money coming in, and what more could Rosaleen ask?

He was not unhappy over his first wife's death a few years after they left England, because they had never really liked each other, and it seemed to him now that even before she was dead he had made up his mind, if she did die, never to marry again. He had held out on this until he was nearly fifty, when he met Rosaleen at a dance in the County Sligo hall far over on East 86th Street. She was a great tall rosy girl, a prize dancer, and the boys were fairly fighting over her. She led him a dance then for two years before she would have him. She said there was nothing against him except he came from Bristol, and the outland Irish had the name of people you couldn't trust. She couldn't say why—it was just a name they had, worse than Dublin people itself. No decent Sligo girl would marry a Dublin man if he was the last man on earth. Dennis didn't believe this, he'd never heard any such thing against the Dubliners; he thought a country girl would lep at the chance to marry a city man whatever. Rosaleen said, "Maybe," but he'd see whether she would lep to marry Bristol Irish. She was chambermaid in a rich woman's house, a fiend of darkness if there ever was one, said Rosaleen, and at first Dennis had been uneasy about the whole thing, fearing a young girl who had to work so hard might be marrying an older man for his money, but before the two years were up he had got over that notion.

It wasn't long after they were married Dennis began almost to wish sometimes he had let one of those strong-armed boys have her, but he had been fond of her, she was a fine good girl, and after she cooled down a little, he knew he could have never done better. The only thing was, he wished it had been Rosaleen he had married that first time in Bristol, and now they'd be settled together, nearer an age. Thirty years was too much difference altogether. But he never said any such thing to Rosaleen. A man owes something to himself. He knocked out his pipe on the foot scraper and felt a real need to go in the kitchen and find a pipe cleaner.

Rosaleen said, "Come in and welcome!" He stood peering around wondering what she had been making. She warned him: "I'm off to milk now, and mind ye keep your eyes in your pocket. The cow now—the creature! Pretty soon she'll be jumping the stone walls after the apples, and running wild through the fields roaring, and it's all for another calf only, the poor deceived thing!" Dennis said, "I don't see what deceit there is in that." "Oh, don't you now?" said Rosaleen, and gathered up her milk pails.

The kitchen was warm and Dennis felt at home again. The kettle was simmering for tea, the cats lay curled on sprawled as they chose, and Dennis sat within himself smiling a sunken smile, cleaning his pipe. In the barn Rosaleen looped up her purple gingham skirts and sat with her forehead pressed against the warm, calm side of the cow, drawing two thick streams of milk into the pail. She said to the cow: "It's no life, no life at all. A man of his years is no comfort to a woman," and went on with a slow murmur that was not complaining about the things of her life.

She wished sometimes they had never come to Connecticut where there was nobody to talk to but Rooshans and Polacks and Wops no better than Black Protestants when you come right down to it. And the natives were worse even. A picture of her neighbors up the hill came into her mind: a starved-looking woman in a blackish gray dress, and a jaundiced man with red-rimmed eyes, and their mizzle-witted boy. On Sundays they shambled by in their sad old shoes, walking to the meeting-house, but that was all the religion they had, thought Rosaleen, contemptuously. On week days they beat the poor boy and the animals, and fought between themselves. Never a feast-day, nor a bit of bright color in their clothes, nor a Christian look out of their eyes for a living soul. "It's just living in mortal sin from one day to the next," said Rosaleen. But it was Dennis getting old that took the heart out of her. And him with the grandest head of hair she had ever seen on a man. A fine man, oh, a fine man Dennis was in those days! Dennis rose before her eyes in his black suit and white gloves, a knowledgeable man who could tell the richest people the right things to order for a good dinner, such a gentleman in his stiff white shirt front, managing the waiters on the one hand and the customers on the other, and making good money at it. And now. No, she couldn't believe it was Dennis any more. Where was Dennis now? and where was Kevin? She was sorry now she had spited Kevin about his girl. It had been all in fun, really, no harm meant. It was strange if you couldn't speak your heart out to a good friend. Kevin had showed her the picture of his girl, like a clap of thunder it came one day when Rosaleen hadn't even heard there was one. She was a waitress in New York, and if ever Rosaleen had laid eyes on a brassy, bold-faced hussy, the kind the boys make jokes about at home, the kind that comes out to New York and goes wrong, this was the one. "You're never never keeping steady with her, are you?" Rosaleen had cried out and the tears came into her eyes. "And why not?" asked Kevin, his chin square as a box. "We've been great now for three years. Who says a word against her says it against me." And there they were, not exactly quarreling, but not friends for the moment, certainly, with Kevin putting the picture back in his pocket, saying: "There's the last of it between us. I was greatly wrong to tell ye!"

That night he was packing up his clothes before he went to bed, but came down and sat on the steps with them awhile, and they made it up by saying nothing, as if nothing had happened. "A man must do something with his life," Kevin explained. "There's always a place to be made in the world, and I'm off to New York, or Boston, maybe." Rosaleen said, "Write me a letter, don't forget, I'll be waiting." "The very day I know where I'll be," he promised her. They had parted with false wide smiles on their faces, arms around each other to the very gate. There had come a postcard from New York of the Woolworth building, with a word on it: "This is my hotel. Kevin." And never another word for these five years. The wretch, the stump! After he had disappeared down the road with his suitcase strapped on his shoulders, Rosaleen had gone back in the house and had looked at herself in the square looking-glass beside the kitchen window. There was a ripple in the glass and a crack across the middle, and it was like seeing your face in water. "Before God I don't look like that," she said, hanging it on the nail again. "If I did, it's no wonder he was leaving. But I don't." She knew in her heart no good would come of him running off after that common-looking girl; but it was likely he'd find her out soon, and come back, for Kevin was nobody's fool. She waited and watched for Kevin to come back and confess she had been right, and he would say, "I'm sorry I hurt your feelings over somebody not fit to look at you!" But now it was five years. She hung a drapery of crochet lace over the frame on the Billy-cat's picture, and propped it up on a small table in the kitchen, and sometimes it gave her an excuse to mention Kevin's name again, though the sound of it was a crack on the eardrums to Dennis. "Don't speak of him," said Dennis, more than once. "He owed it to send us word. It's ingratitude I can't stand." Whatever was she going to do with Dennis now, she wondered, and sighed heavily into the flank of the cow. It wasn't being a wife at all to wrap a man in flannels like a baby and put hot water bottles to him. She got up sighing and kicked back the stool. "There you are now," she said to the cow.

She couldn't help feeling happy all at once at the sight of the lamp and the fire making everything cozy, and the smell of vanilla reminded her of perfume. She set the table with a white-fringed cloth while Dennis strained the milk.

"Now, Dennis, today's a big day, and we're having a feast for it."

"Is it All-Saints?" asked Dennis, who never looked at a calendar any more. What's a day, more or less?

"It is not," said Rosaleen; "draw up your chair now."

Dennis made another guess it was Christmas, and Rosaleen said it was a better day than Christmas, even.

"I can't think what," said Dennis, looking at the glossy baked goose. "It's nobody's birthday that I mind."

Rosaleen lifted the cake like a mound of new snow blooming with candles. "Count them and see what day is this, will you?" she urged him.

Dennis counted them with a waggling forefinger. "So it is, Rosaleen, so it is."

They went on bandying words. It had slipped his mind entirely. Rosaleen wanted to know when hadn't it slipped his mind? For all he ever thought of it, they might never have had a wedding day at all. "That's not so," said Dennis. "I mind well I married you. It's the date that slips me."

"You might as well be English," said Rosaleen, "you might just as well."

She glanced at the clock, and reminded him it was twenty-five years ago that morning at ten o'clock, and tonight the very hour they had sat down to their first married dinner together. Dennis thought maybe it was telling people what to eat and then watching them eat it all those years that had taken away his wish for food.

"You know I can't eat cake," he said. "It upsets my stomach."

Rosaleen felt sure her cake wouldn't upset the stomach of a nursing child. Dennis knew better, any kind of cake sat on him like a stone. While the argument went on, they ate nearly all the goose which fairly melted on the tongue, and finished with wedges of cake and floods of tea, and Dennis had to admit he hadn't felt better in years. He looked at her sitting across the table from him and thought she was a very fine woman, noticed again her red hair and yellow eyelashes and big arms and strong big teeth, and wondered what she thought of him now he was no human good to her. Here he was, all gone, and he had been so for years, and he felt guilt sometimes before Rosaleen, who couldn't always understand how there comes a time when a man is finished, and there is no more to be done that way. Rosaleen poured out two small glasses of home-made cherry brandy.

"I could feel like dancing itself this night, Dennis," she told him. "Do you remember the first time we met in Sligo Hall with the band playing?" She gave him another glass of brandy and took one herself and leaned over with her eyes shining as if she was telling him something he had never heard before.

"I remember a boy in Ireland was a great step-dancer,

the best, and he was wild about me and I was a devil to him. Now what makes a girl like that, Dennis? He was a fine match, too, all the girls were glad of a chance with him, but I wasn't. He said to me a thousand times, 'Rosaleen, why won't ye dance with me just once?' And I'd say, 'Ye've plenty to dance with ye without my wasting my time.' And so it went for the summer long with him not dancing at all and everybody plaguing the living life out of him, till in the end I danced with him. Afterwards he walked home with me and a crowd of them, and there was a heaven full of stars and the dogs barking far off. Then I promised to keep steady with him, and was sorry for it the minute I promised. I was like that. We used to be the whole day getting ready for the dances, washing our hair and curling it and trying on our dresses and trimming them, laughing fit to kill about the boys and making up things to say to them. When my sister Honora was married they took me for the bride, Dennis, with my white dress ruffled to the heels and my hair with a wreath. Everybody drank my health for the belle of the ball, and said I would surely be the next bride. Honora said for me to save my blushes or I'd have none left for my own wedding. She was always jealous, Dennis, she's jealous of me to this day, you know that."

"Maybe so," said Dennis.

"There's no maybe about it," said Rosaleen. "But **we had** grand times together when we was little. I mind the time when my great-grandfather was ninety years old and on his deathbed. We watched by turns the night—"

"And he was a weary time on it," said Dennis, to show his interest. He was so sleepy he could hardly hold up his head.

"He was," said Rosaleen, "so this night Honora and me was watching, and we was yawning our hearts out of us, for there had been a great ball the night before. Our mother told us, 'Feel his feet from time to time, and when you feel the chill rising, you'll know he's near the end. He can't last out the night,' she said, 'but stay by him.' So there we was drinking tea and laughing to-gether in whispers to keep awake, and the old man lying there with his chin propped on the quilt. 'Wait a minute,' says Honora, and she felt his feet. 'They're getting cold,' she says, and went on telling me what she had said to Shane at the ball, how he was jealous of Terence and asks her can he trust her out of his sight. And Honora says to Shane, 'No, you cannot,' and oh, but he was roaring mad with anger! Then Honora stuffs her fist in her mouth to keep down the giggles. I felt great-grand-father's feet and legs and they was like clay to the knees, and I says, 'Maybe we'd better call somebody'; but Honora says, 'Oh, there's a power of him left to get cold yet!' So we poured out tea and began to comb and braid each other's hair, and fell to whispering our secrets and laughing more. Then Honora put her hand under the quilt and said, 'Rosaleen, his stomach's cold, it's gone he must be by now.' Then great-grandfather opened the one eye full of rage and says, 'It's nothing of the kind, and to hell with ye!' We let out a great scream, and the others came flying in, and Honora cried out, 'Oh, he's dead and gone surely, God rest him!' And would you believe it, it was so. He was gone. And while the old women were washing him Honora and me sat down laughing and crying in the one breath . . . and it was six months later to the very day great-grandfather came to me in the dream, the way I told you, and he was still after Honora and me for laughing in the watch. 'I've a great mind to thrash ye within an inch of your life,' he told me, 'only I'm wailing in Purgatory this minute for them last words to ye. Go and have an extra Mass said for the repose of me soul because it's by your misconduct I'm here at all,' he says to me. 'Get a move on now,' he said. 'And be damned to ye!'"

"And you woke up in a sweat," said Dennis, "and was off to Mass before daybreak."

Rosaleen nodded her head. "Ah, Dennis, if I'd set my heart on that boy I need never have left Ireland. And when I think how it all came out with him. With me so far away, him struck on the head and left for dead in a ditch."

"You dreamed that," said Dennis.

"Surely I dreamed it, and it is so. When I was crying and crying over him—" Rosaleen was proud of her crying—"I didn't know then what good luck I would find here."

Dennis couldn't think what good luck she was talking about.

"Let it pass, then," said Rosaleen. She went to the corner shelves again. "The man today was selling pipes," she said, "and I bought the finest he had." It was an imitation meerschaum pipe carved with a crested lion glaring out of a jungle and it was as big as a man's fist.

Dennis said, "You must have paid a pretty penny for that."

"It doesn't concern ye," said Rosaleen. "I wanted to give ye a pipe."

Dennis said, "It's grand carving, I wonder if it'll draw at all." He filled it and lit it and said there wasn't much taste on a new one, for he was tired holding it up.

"It is such a pipe as my father had once," Rosaleen said to encourage him. "And in no time it was fit to knock ye off your feet, he said. So it will be a fine pipe some day."

"And some day I'll be in my tomb," thought Dennis,

bitterly, "and she'll find a man can keep her quiet."

When they were in bed Rosaleen took his head on her shoulder. "Dennis, I could cry for the wink of an eyelash. When I think how happy we were that wedding day."

"From the way you carried on," said Dennis, feeling very sly all of a sudden on that brandy, "I thought different."

"Go to sleep," said Rosaleen, prudishly. "That's no way to talk."

Dennis's head fell back like a bag of sand on the pillow. Rosaleen could not sleep, and lay thinking about marriage: not about her own, for once you've given your word there's nothing to think about in it, but all other kinds of marriages, unhappy ones: where the husband drinks, or won't work, or mistreats his wife and the children. Where the wife runs away from home, or spoils the children or neglects them, or turns a perfect strumpet and flirts with other men: where a woman marries a man too young for her, and he feels cheated and strays after other women till it's just a disgrace: or take when a young girl marries an old man, even if he has money she's bound to be disappointed in some way. If Dennis hadn't been such a good man, God knows what might have come out of it. She was lucky. It would break your heart to dwell on it. Her black mood closed down on her and she wanted to walk the floor holding her head and remembering every unhappy thing in the world. She had had nothing but disasters, one after another, and she couldn't get over them, no matter how long ago they happened. Once she had let entirely the wrong man kiss her, she had almost got into bad trouble with him, and even now her heart stopped on her when she thought how near she'd come to being a girl with no character. There was the Billy-cat and his good heart and his sad death, and it was mixed up with the time her father had been knocked down, by a runaway horse, when the drink was in him, and the time when she had to wear mended stockings to a big ball because that sneaky Honora had stolen the only good ones.

She wished now she'd had a dozen children instead of the one that died in two days. This half-forgotten child suddenly lived again in her, she began to weep for him with all the freshness of her first agony; now he would be a fine grown man and the dear love of her heart. The image of him floated before her eyes plain as day, and became Kevin, painting the barn and the pig sty all colors of the rainbow, the brush swinging in his hand like a bell. He would work like a wild man for days and then lie for days under the trees, idle as a tramp. The darling, the darling lad like her own son. A painter by trade was a nice living, but she couldn't bear the thought

of him boarding around the country with the heathen
Rooshans and Polacks and Wops with their liquor stills
and their outlandish lingo. She said as much to Kevin.

"It's not a Christian way to live, and you a good
County Sligo boy."

So Kevin started to make jokes at her like any other
Sligo boy. "I said to myself, that's a County Mayo
woman if ever I clapped eyes on one."

"Hold your tongue," said Rosaleen softly as a dove.
"You're talking to a Sligo woman as if you didn't know
it!"

"Is it so?" said Kevin in great astonishment. "Well,
I'm glad of the mistake. The Mayo people are too proud
for me."

"And for me, too," said Rosaleen. "They beat the
world for holding up their chins about nothing."

"They do so," said Kevin, "but the Sligo people have
a right to be proud."

"And you've a right to live in a good Irish house,"
said Rosaleen, "so you'd best come with us."

"I'd be proud of that as if I came from Mayo," said
Kevin, and he went on slapping paint on Rosaleen's
front gate. They stood there smiling at each other, feeling they had agreed enough, it was time to think of how
to get the best of each other in the talk from now on.

For more than a year they had tried to get the best of each other in the talk, and sometimes it was one and sometimes another, but a gay easy time and such a bubble of joy like a kettle singing. "You've been a sister to me, Rosaleen, I'll not forget ye while I have breath," he had said that the last night.

Dennis muttered and snored a little. Rosaleen wanted to mourn about everything at the top of her voice, but it wouldn't do to wake Dennis. He was sleeping like the dead after all that goose.

Rosaleen said, "Dennis, I dreamed about Kevin in the night. There was a grave, an old one, but with fresh flowers on it, and a name on the headstone cut very clear but as if it was in another language and I couldn't make it out some way. You came up then and I said, 'Dennis, what grave is this?' and you answered me, 'That's Kevin's grave, don't you remember? And you put those flowers there yourself.' Then I said, 'Well, a grave it is then, and let's not think of it any more.' Now isn't it strange to think Kevin's been dead all this time and I didn't know it?"

Dennis said, "He's not fit to mention, going off as he did after all our kindness to him, and not a word from him."

184

"It was because he hadn't the power any more," said Rosaleen. "And ye mustn't be down on him now. I was wrong to put my judgment on him the way I did. Ah, but to think! Kevin dead and gone, and all these natives and foreigners living on, with the paint still on their barns and houses where Kevin put it! It's very bitter."

Grieving for Kevin, she drifted into thinking of the natives and foreigners who owned farms all around her. She was afraid for her life of them, she said, the way they looked at you out of their heathen faces, the foreigners bold as brass, the natives sly and mean. "The way they do be selling the drink to all, and burning each other in their beds and splitting each other's heads with axes," she complained. "The decent people aren't safe in their houses."

Yesterday she had seen that native Guy Richards going by wild-drunk again, fit to do any crime. He was a great offense to Rosaleen, with his shaggy mustaches and his shirt in rags till the brawny skin showed through; a shame to the world, staring around with his sneering eyes; living by himself in a shack and having his cronies in for drink until you could hear them shouting at all hours and careering round the countryside like the devils from hell. He would pass by the house driving his bony gray horse at top speed, standing up in the rackety buggy singing in a voice like a power of scrap-iron falling, drunk as a lord before breakfast. Once when Rosaleen was standing in her doorway, wearing a green checkerboard dress, he yelled at her: "Hey, Rosie, want to come for a ride?"

"The bold stump!" said Rosaleen to Dennis. "If ever he lays a finger on me I'll shoot him dead."

"If you mind your business by day," said Dennis in a shriveled voice, "and bar the doors well by night, there'll be no call to shoot anybody."

"Little you know!" said Rosaleen. She had a series of visions of Richards laying a finger on her and herself shooting him dead in his tracks. "Whatever would I do without ye, Dennis?" she asked him that night, as they sat on the steps in a soft darkness full of fireflies and the sound of crickets. "When I think of all the kinds of men there are in the world. That Richards!"

"When a man is young he likes his fun," said Dennis, amiably, beginning to yawn.

"Young, is it?" said Rosaleen, warm with anger. "The old crow! Fit to have children grown he is, the same as myself, and I'm a settled woman over her nonsense!"

Dennis almost said, "I'll never call you old," but all at once he was irritable too. "Will you stop your gossiping?" he asked censoriously.

Rosaleen sat silent, without rancor, but there was no denying the old man was getting old, old. He got up as if he gathered his bones in his arms, and carried himself in the house. Somewhere inside of him there must be Dennis, but where? "The world is a wilderness," she informed the crickets and frogs and fireflies.

Richards never had offered to lay a finger on Rosaleen, but now and again he pulled up at the gate when he was not quite drunk, and sat with them afternoons on the doorstep, and there were signs in him of a nice-behaved man before the drink got him down. He would tell them stories of his life, and what a desperate wild fellow he had been, all in all. Not when he was a boy, though. As long as his mother lived he had never done a thing to hurt her feelings. She wasn't what you might call a rugged woman, the least thing made her sick, and she was so religious she prayed all day long under her breath at her work, and even while she ate. He had belonged to a society called The Sons of Temperance, with all the boys in the countryside banded together under a vow never to touch strong drink in any form: "Not even for medicinal purposes," he would quote, raising his right arm and staring solemnly before him. Quite often he would burst into a rousing march tune which he remembered from the weekly singings they had held: "With flags of temperance flying, With banners white as snow," and he could still repeat almost word for word the favorite poem he had been called upon to recite at every meeting: "At midnight, in his guarded tent, The Turk lay dreaming of the hour—"

Rosaleen wanted to interrupt sometimes and tell him that had been no sort of life, he should have been young in Ireland. But she wouldn't say it. She sat stiffly beside Dennis and looked at Richards severely out of the corner of her eye, wondering if he remembered that time he had yelled "Hey, Rosie!" at her. It was enough to make a woman wild not to find a word in her mouth for such boldness. The cheek of him, pretending nothing had happened. One day she was racking her mind for some saying that would put him in his place, while he was telling about the clambakes his gang was always having down by the creek behind the rock pile, with a keg of home-brew beer; and the dances the Railroad Street out-fit gave every Saturday night in Winston. "We're always up to some devilment," he said, looking straight at Rosaleen, and before she could say scat, the hellion had winked his near eye at her. She turned away with her mouth down at the corners; after a long minute, she said, "Good day to ye, Mr. Richards," cold as ice, and went in the house. She took down the looking-glass to see what kind of look she had on her, but the wavy place made her eyes broad and blurred as the palm of her hands, and she couldn't tell her nose from her mouth in the cracked seam. . . .

The pipe salesman came back next month and brought a patent cooking pot that cooked vegetables perfectly without any water in them. "It's a lot healthier way of cooking, Miz O'Toole," Dennis heard his mouthy voice going thirteen to the dozen. "I'm telling you as a friend because you're a good customer of mine."

"Is it so?" thought Dennis, and his gall stirred within him.

"You'll find it's going to be a perfect godsend for your husband's health. Old folks need to be mighty careful what they eat, and you know better than I do, Miz O'Toole, that health begins or ends right in the kitchen. Now your husband don't look as stout as he might. It's because, tasty as your cooking is, you've been pouring all the good vitamins, the sunlit life-giving elements, right down the sink . . . Right down the sink, Miz O'Toole, is where you're pouring your husband's health and your own. And I say it's a shame, a good-looking woman like you wasting your time and strength standing over a cook-stove when all you've got to do from now on is just fill this scientific little contrivance with whatever you've planned for dinner and then go away and read a good book in your parlor while it's cooking,— or curl your hair."

"My hair curls by nature," said Rosaleen. Dennis almost groaned aloud from his hiding-place.

"For the love of—why, Miz O'Toole, you don't mean to tell me that! When I first saw that hair, I said to myself, why, it's so perfect it looks to be artificial! I was just getting ready to ask you how you did it so I could tell my wife. Well, if your hair curls like that, without any vitamins at all, I want to come back and have a look at it after you've been cooking in this little pot for two weeks."

Rosaleen said, "Well, it's not my looks I'm thinking about. But my husband isn't up to himself, and that's the truth, Mr. Pendleton. Ah, it would have done your heart good to see that man in his younger days! Strong as an ox he was, the way no man dared to rouse his anger. I've seen my husband, many's the time, swing on a man with his fist and send him sprawling twenty feet, and that for the least thing, mind you! But Dennis could never hold his grudge for long, and the next instant you'd see him picking the man up and dusting him off like a brother and saying, 'Now think no more of that.' He was too forgiving always. It was his great fault."

"And look at him now," said Mr. Pendleton, sadly.

Dennis felt pretty hot around the ears. He stood forward at the corner of the house, listening. He had never weighed more than one hundred thirty pounds at his most, a tall thin man he had been always, a little proud

of his elegant shape, and not since he left school in
Bristol had he lifted his hand in anger against a creature,
brute or human. "He was a fine man a woman could rely
on, Mr. Pendleton," said Rosaleen, "and quick as a
tiger with his fists."

"I might be dead and moldering away to dust the
way she talks," thought Dennis, "and there she is throwing away the money as if she was already a gay widow
woman." He tottered out bent on speaking his mind and
putting a stop to such foolishness. The salesman turned
a floppy smile and shrewd little eyes upon him. "Hello,
Mr. O'Toole," he said, with the manly cordiality he
used for husbands. "I'm just leaving you a little birthday
present with the Missis here."

"It's not my birthday," said Dennis, sour as a lemon.

"That's just a manner of speaking!" interrupted
Rosaleen, merrily. "And now many thanks to ye, Mr.
Pendleton."

"Many thanks to *you*, Miz O'Toole," answered the
salesman, folding away nine dollars of good green
money. No more was said except good day, and Rosaleen stood shading her eyes to watch the Ford wallop-
ing off down the hummocky lane. "That's a nice, decent
family man," she told Dennis, as if rebuking his evil
thoughts. "He travels out of New York, and he always
has the latest thing and the best. He's full of admiration

for ye, too, Dennis. He said he couldn't call to mind another man of your age as sound as you are."

"I heard him," said Dennis. "I know all he said."

"Well, then," said Rosaleen, serenely, "there's no good saying it over." She hurried to wash potatoes to cook in the pot that made the hair curl.

The winter piled in upon them, and the snow was shot through with blizzards. Dennis couldn't bear a breath of cold, and all but sat in the oven, rheumy and grunty, with his muffler on. Rosaleen began to feel as if she couldn't bear her clothes on her in the hot kitchen, and when she did the barn work she had one chill after another. She complained that her hands were gnawed to the bone with the cold. Did Dennis realize that now, or was he going to sit like a log all winter, and where was the lad he had promised her to help with the outside work?

Dennis sat wordless under her unreasonableness, thinking she had very little work for a strong-bodied woman, and the truth was she was blaming him for something he couldn't help. Still she said nothing he could take hold of, only nipping his head off when the kettle dried up or the fire went low. There would come a day when she would say outright, "It's no life here, I won't stay here any longer," and she would drag him back to a flat in New York, or even leave him, maybe. Would she? Would she do such a thing? Such a thought had never occurred to him before. He peered at her as if he watched her through a keyhole. He tried to think of something to ease her mind, but no plan came. She would look at some harmless thing around the house, say—the calendar, and suddenly tear it off the wall and stuff it in the fire. "I hate the very sight of it," she would explain, and she was always hating the very sight of one thing or another, even the cow; almost, but not quite, the cats.

One morning she sat up very tired and forlorn, and began almost before Dennis could get an eye open: "I had a dream in the night that my sister Honora was sick and dying in her bed, and was calling for me." She bowed her head on her hands and breathed brokenly to her very toes, and said, "It's only natural I must go to Boston to find out for myself how it is, isn't it?"

Dennis, pulling on his chest protector she had knitted him for Christmas, said, "I suppose so. It looks that way."

Over the coffee pot she began making her plans. "I could go if only I had a coat. It should be a fur one against this weather. A coat is what I've needed all these years. If I had a coat I'd go this very day."

"You've a greatcoat with fur on it," said Dennis.

"A rag of a coat!" cried Rosaleen. "And I won't have Honora see me in it. She was jealous always, Dennis, she'd be glad to see me without a coat."

"If she's sick and dying maybe she won't notice," said Dennis.

Rosaleen agreed. "And maybe it will be better to buy one there, or in New York—something in the new style."

"It's long out of your way by New York," said Dennis. "There's shorter ways to Boston than that."

"It's by New York I'm going, because the trains are better," said Rosaleen, "and I want to go that way." There was a look on her face as if you could put her on the rack and she wouldn't yield. Dennis kept silence.

When the postman passed she asked him to leave word with the native family up the hill to send their lad down for a few days to help with the chores, at the same pay as before. And tomorrow morning, if it was all the same to him, she'd be driving in with him to the train. All day long, with her hair in curl papers, she worked getting her things together in the lazy old canvas bag. She put a ham on to bake and set bread and filled the closet off the kitchen with firewood. "Maybe there'll come a message saying Honora's better and I sha'n't have to go," she said several times, but her eyes were excited and she walked about so briskly the floor shook.

Late in the afternoon Guy Richards knocked, and floundered in stamping his big boots. He was almost sober, but he wasn't going to be for long. Rosaleen said, "I've sad news about my sister, she's on her deathbed maybe and I'm going to Boston."

"I hope it's nothing serious, Missis O'Toole," said Richards. "Let's drink her health in this," and he took out a bottle half full of desperate-looking drink. Dennis said he didn't mind. Richards said, "Will the lady join us?" and his eyes had the devil in them if Rosaleen had ever seen it.

"I will not," she said. "I've something better to do."

While they drank she sat fixing the hem of her dress, and began to tell again about the persons without number she'd known who came back from the dead to bring word about themselves, and Dennis himself would back her up in it. She told again the story of the Billy-cat, her voice warm and broken with the threat of tears.

Dennis swallowed his drink, leaned over and began to fumble with his shoelace, his face sunken to a handful of wrinkles, and thought right out plainly to himself: "There's not a word of truth in it, not a word. And she'll go on telling it to the world's end for God's truth." He felt helpless, as if he were involved in some disgraceful fraud. He wanted to speak up once for all and say, "It's a lie, Rosaleen, it's something you've made up, and now let's hear no more about it." But Richards, sitting there with his ears lengthened, stopped the words in Dennis's throat. The moment passed. Rosaleen said solemnly, "My dreams never renege on me, Mr. Richards. They're all I have to go by." "It never happened at all," said Dennis inside himself, stubbornly. "Only the Billy-cat got caught in a trap and I buried him." Could this really have been all? He had a nightmarish feeling that somewhere just out of his reach lay the truth about it, he couldn't swear for certain, yet he was *almost* willing to swear that this had been all. Richards got up saying he had to be getting on to a shindig at Winston. "I'll take you to the train tomorrow, Missis O'Toole," he said. "I love doing a good turn for the ladies."

Rosaleen said very stiffly, "I'll be going in with the letter-carrier, and many thanks just the same."

She tucked Dennis into bed with great tenderness and sat by him a few minutes, putting cold cream on her face. "It won't be for long," she told him, "and you're well taken care of the whole time. Maybe by the grace of God I'll find her recovered."

"Maybe she's not sick at all," Dennis wanted to say, and said instead, "I hope so." It was nothing to him. Everything else aside, it seemed a great fuss to be making over Honora, who might die when she liked for all Dennis would turn a hair.

Dennis hoped until the last minute that Rosaleen would come to her senses and give up the trip, but at the last minute there she was with her hat and the rag of a coat, a streak of pink powder on her chin, pulling on her tan gloves that smelt of naphtha, flourishing a handkerchief that smelt of Azurea, and going every minute to the window, looking for the postman. "In this snow maybe he'll be late," she said in a trembling voice. "What if he didn't come at all?" She took a last glimpse at herself in the mirror. "One thing I must remember, Dennis," she said in another tone. "And that is, to bring back a looking-glass that won't make my face look like a monster's."

"It's a good enough glass," said Dennis, "without throwing away money."

The postman came only a few minutes late. Dennis kissed Rosaleen good-by and shut the kitchen door so he could not see her climbing into the car, but he heard her laughing.

"It's just a born liar she is," Dennis said to himself, sitting by the stove, and at once he felt he had leaped head-first into a very dark pit. His better self tried to argue it out with him. "Have you no shame," said Dennis's better self, "thinking such thoughts about your own wife?" The baser Dennis persisted. "It's not half she deserves," he answered sternly, "leaving me here by my lone, and for what?" That was the great question. Certainly not to run after Honora, living or dying or dead. Where then? For what on earth? Here he stopped thinking altogether. There wasn't a spark in his mind. He had a lump on his chest that could surely be pneumonia if he had a cold, which he hadn't, specially. His feet ached until you'd swear it was rheumatism, only he never had it. Still, he wasn't thinking. He stayed in this condition for two days, and the under-witted lad from the native farm above did all the work, even to washing the dishes. Dennis ate pretty well, considering the grief he was under.

Rosaleen settled back in the plush seat and thought how she had always been a great traveler. A train was like home to her, with all the other people sitting near, and the smell of newspapers and some kind of nice-smelling furniture polish and the perfume from fur collars, and the train dust and something over and above she couldn't place, but it was the smell of travel: fruit, maybe, or was it machinery? She bought chocolate bars, though she wasn't hungry, and a magazine of love stories, though she was never one for reading. She only wished to prove to herself she was once more on a train going somewhere.

She watched the people coming on or leaving at the stations, greeting, or kissing good-by, and it seemed a lucky sign she did not see a sad face anywhere. There was a cold sweet sunshine on the snow, and the city people didn't look all frozen and bundled up. Their faces looked smooth after the gnarled raw frost-bitten country faces. The Grand Central hadn't changed at all, with all the crowds whirling in every direction, and a noise that almost had a tune in it, it was so steady. She held on to her bag the colored men were trying to get away from her, and stood on the sidewalk trying to remember which direction was Broadway where the moving pictures were. She hadn't seen one for five years, it was high time now! She wished she had an hour to visit her old flat in 164th Street—just a turn around the block would be enough, but there wasn't time. An old resentment rose against Honora, who was a born spoil-sport and would spoil this trip for her if she could. She walked on, getting her directions, brooding a little because she had been such a city girl once, thinking only of dress and a good time, and now she hardly knew one street from another. She went into the first moving-picture theater she saw because she liked the name of it. "The Prince of Love," she said to herself. It was about two beautiful young things, a boy with black wavy hair and a girl with curly golden hair, who loved each other and had great troubles, but it all came well in the end, and all the time it was just one fine ballroom or garden after another, and such beautiful clothes! She sniffled a little in the Azurea-smelling handkerchief, and ate her chocolates, and reminded herself these two were really alive and looked just like that, but it was hard to believe living beings could be so beautiful.

After the dancing warm lights of the screen the street was cold and dark and ugly, with the slush and the roar and the millions of people all going somewhere in a great rush, but not one face she knew. She decided to go to Boston by boat the way she used in the old days when she visited Honora. She gazed into the shop windows thinking how the styles in underthings had changed till she could hardly believe her eyes, wondering what Dennis would say if she bought the green glove silk slip with the tea-colored lace. Ah, was he eating his ham now as she told him, and did the boy come to help as he had promised?

She ate ice cream with strawberry preserves on it, and bought a powder puff and decided there was time for another moving picture. It was called "The Lover King," and it was about a king in a disguise, a lovely young man with black wavy hair and eyes would melt in his head, who married a poor country girl who was more beautiful than all the princesses and ladies in the land. Music came out of the screen, and voices talking, and Rosaleen cried, for the love songs went to her heart like a dagger.

Afterward there was just time to ride in a taxi to Christopher Street and catch the boat. She felt happier the minute she set foot on board, how she always loved a ship! She ate her supper thinking, "That boy didn't have much style to his waiting. Dennis would never have kept him on in the hotel"; and afterward sat in the lounge and listened to the radio until she almost fell asleep there before everybody. She stretched out in her narrow bunk and felt the engine pounding under her, and the grand steady beat shook the very marrow of her bones. The fog horn howled and bellowed through the darkness over the rush of water, and Rosaleen turned on her side. "Howl for me, that's the way I could cry in the nighttime in that lost heathen place," for Connecticut seemed a thousand miles and a hundred years away by now. She fell asleep and had no dreams at all.

In the morning she felt this was a lucky sign. At Providence she took the train again, and as the meeting with Honora came nearer, she grew sunken and tired. "Always Honora making trouble," she thought, standing outside the station holding her bag and thinking it strange she hadn't remembered what a dreary ugly place Boston was; she couldn't remember any good times there. Taxicab drivers were yelling in her face. Maybe it would be a good thing to go to a church and light a candle for Honora. The taxi scampered through winding streets to the nearest church, with Rosaleen thinking, what she wouldn't give to be able to ride around all day, and never walk at all!

She knelt near the high altar, and something surged up in her heart and pushed the tears out of her eyes. Prayers began to tumble over each other on her lips. How long it had been since she had seen the church as it should be, dressed for a feast with candles and flowers, smelling of incense and wax. The little doleful church in Winston, now who could really pray in it? "Have mercy on us," said Rosaleen, calling on fifty saints at once; "I confess . . ." she struck her breast three times, then got up suddenly, carrying her bag, and peered into the confessionals hoping she might find a priest in one of them. "It's too early, or it's not the day, but I'll come back," she promised herself with tenderness. She lit the candle for Honora and went away feeling warm and quiet. She was blind and confused, too, and could not make up her mind what to do next. Where ever should she turn? It was a burning sin to spend money on taxicabs when there was always the hungry poor in the world, but she hailed one anyhow, and gave Honora's house number. Yes, there it was, just like in old times.

She read all the names pasted on slips above the bells, all the floors front and back, but Honora's name was not among them. The janitor had never heard of Mrs. Terence Gogarty, nor Mrs. Honora Gogarty, neither. Maybe it would be in the telephone book. There were many Gogartys but no Terence nor Honora. Rosaleen smothered down the impulse to tell the janitor, a good Irishman, how her dream had gone back on her. "Thank ye kindly, it's no great matter," she said, and stepped out into the street again. The wind hacked at her shoulders through the rag of a coat, the bag was too heavy altogether. Now what kind of nature was in Honora not to drop a line and say she had moved?

Walking about with her mind in a whirl, she came to a small dingy square with iron benches and some naked trees in it. Sitting, she began to shed tears again. When one handkerchief was wet she took out another, and the fresh perfume put new heart in her. She glanced around when a shadow fell on the corner of her eye, and there hunched on the other end of the bench was a scrap of a lad with freckles, his collar turned about his ears, his red hair wilted on his forehead under his bulging cap. He slanted his gooseberry eyes at her and said, "We've all something to cry for in this world, isn't it so?"

Rosaleen said, "I'm crying because I've come a long way for nothing."

The boy said, "I knew you was a County Sligo woman the minute I clapped eyes on ye."

"God bless ye for that," said Rosaleen, "for I am."

"I'm County Sligo myself, long ago, and curse the day I ever thought of leaving it," said the boy, with such anger Rosaleen dried her eyes once for all and turned to have a good look at him.

"Whatever makes ye say that now?" she asked him. "It's a good country, this. There's opportunity for all here."

"So I've heard tell many's the countless times," said the boy. "There's all the opportunity in the wide world to shrivel with the hunger and walk the soles off your boots hunting the work, and there's a great chance of dying in the gutter at last. God forgive me the first thought I had of coming here."

"Ye haven't been out long?" asked Rosaleen.

"Eleven months and five days the day," said the boy. He plunged his hands into his pockets and stared at the freezing mud clotted around his luckless shoes.

"And what might ye do by way of a living?" asked Rosaleen.

"I'm an hostler," he said. "I used to work at the Dublin race tracks, even. No man can tell me about horses," he said proudly. "And it's good work if it's to be found."

Rosaleen looked attentively at his sharp red nose, frozen it was, and the stung look around his eyes, and the sharp bones sticking out at his wrists, and was surprised at herself for thinking, in the first glance, that he had the look of Kevin. She saw different now, but think if it had been Kevin! Better off to be dead and gone. "I'm perishing of hunger and cold," she told him, "and if I knew where there was a place to eat, we'd have some lunch, for it's late."

His eyes looked like he was drowning. "Would ye? I know a place!" and he leaped up as if he meant to run. They did almost run to the edge of the square and the far corner. It was a Coffee Pot and full of the smell of hot cakes. "We'll get our fill here," said Rosaleen, taking off her gloves, "though I'd never call it a grand place."

The boy ate one thing after another as if he could never stop: roast beef and potatoes and spaghetti and custard pie and coffee, and Rosaleen ordered a package of cigarettes. It was like this with her, she was fond of the smell of tobacco, her husband was a famous smoker, never without his pipe. "It's no use keeping it in," said the boy. "I haven't a penny, yesterday and today I didn't eat till now, and I've been fit to hang myself, **or go** to jail for a place to lay my head."

Rosaleen said, "I'm a woman doesn't have to think of money, I have all my heart desires, and a boy like yourself has a right to think nothing of a little loan will never be missed." She fumbled in her purse and brought out a ten-dollar bill, crumpled it and pushed it under the rim of his saucer so the man behind the counter wouldn't notice. "That's for luck in the new world," she said, smiling at him. "You might be Kevin or my own brother, or my own little lad alone in the world, and it'll surely come back to me if ever I need it."

The boy said, "I never thought to see this day," and put the money in his pocket.

Rosaleen said, "I don't even know your name, think of that!"

"I'm a blight on the name of Sullivan," said he. "Hugh it is—Hugh Sullivan."

"That's a good enough name," said Rosaleen. "I've cousins named Sullivan in Dublin, but I never saw one of them. There was a man named Sullivan married my mother's sister, my aunt Brigid she was, and she went to live in Dublin. You're not related to the Dublin Sullivans, are ye?"

"I never heard of it, but maybe I am."

"Ye have the look of a Sullivan to me," said Rosaleen,

"and they're cousins of mine, some of them." She ordered more coffee and he lit another cigarette, and she told him how she had come out more than twenty-five years past, a greenhorn like himself, and everything had turned out well for her and all her family here. Then she told about her husband, how he had been head waiter and a moneyed man, but he was old now; about the farm, if there was someone to help her, they could make a good thing of it; and about Kevin and the way he had gone away and died and sent her news of it in a dream; and this led to the dream about Honora, and here she was, the first time ever a dream had gone back on her. She went on to say there was always room for a strong willing boy in the country if he knew about horses, and how it was a shame for him to be tramping the streets with an empty stomach when there was everything to be had if he only knew which way to look for it. She leaned over and took him by the arm very urgently.

"You've a right to live in a good Irish house," she told him. "Why don't ye come home with me and live there like one of the family in peace and comfort?"

Hugh Sullivan stared at her out of his glazed green eyes down the edge of his sharp nose and a crafty look came over him. " 'Twould be dangerous," he said. "I'd hate to try it."

"Dangerous, is it?" asked Rosaleen. "What danger is there in the peaceful countryside?"

"It's not safe at all," said Hugh. "I was caught at it once in Dublin, and there was a holy row! A fine woman like yourself she was, and her husband peeking through a crack in the wall the whole time. Man, that was a scrape for ye!"

Rosaleen understood in her bones before her mind grasped it. "Whatever—" she began, and the blood boiled up in her face until it was like looking through a red veil. "Ye little whelp," she said, trying to get her breath, "so it's that kind ye are, is it? I might know you're from Dublin! Never in my whole life—" Her rage rose like a bonfire in her, and she stopped. "If I was looking for a man," she said, "I'd choose a *man* and not a half-baked little . . ." She took a deep breath and started again. "The *cheek* of ye," she said, "insulting a woman could be your mother. God keep me from it! It's plain you're just an ignorant greenhorn, doesn't know the ways of decent people, and now be off—" She stood up and motioned to the man behind the counter. "Out of that door now—"

He stood up too, glancing around fearfully with his narrow green eyes, and put out a hand as if he would try to make it up with her. "Not so loud now, woman alive, it's what any man might think the way ye're—"

208

Rosaleen said, "Hold your tongue or I'll tear it out of your head!" and her right arm went back in a business-like way.

He ducked and shot past her, then collected himself and lounged out of reach. "Farewell to ye, County Sligo woman," he said tauntingly. "I'm from County Cork myself!" and darted through the door.

Rosaleen shook so she could hardly find the money for the bill, and she couldn't see her way before her, but when the cold air struck her, her head cleared, and she could have almost put a curse on Honora for making all this trouble for her. . . .

She took a train the short way home, for the taste of travel had soured on her altogether. She wanted to be home and nowhere else. That shameless boy, whatever was he thinking of? "Boys do be known for having evil minds in them," she told herself, and the blood fairly crinkled in her veins. But he had said, "A fine woman like yourself," and maybe he'd met too many bold ones, and thought they were all alike; maybe she had been too free in her ways because he was Irish and looked so sad and poor. But there it was, he was a mean sort, and he would have made love to her if she hadn't stopped him, maybe. It flashed over her and she saw it clear as day—Kevin had loved her all the time, and she had sent him away to that cheap girl who wasn't half good enough for him! And Kevin a sweet decent boy would have cut off his right hand rather than give her an improper word. Kevin had loved her and she had loved Kevin and, oh, she hadn't known it in time! She bowed herself back into the corner with her elbow on the window-sill, her old fur collar pulled up around her face, and wept long and bitterly for Kevin, who would have stayed if she had said the word—and now he was gone and lost and dead. She would hide herself from the world and never speak to a soul again.

"Safe and sound she is, Dennis," Rosaleen told him. "She's been dangerous, but it's past. I left her in health."

"That's good enough," said Dennis, without enthusiasm. He took off his cap with the ear flaps and ran his fingers through his downy white hair and put the cap on again and stood waiting to hear the wonders of the trip; but Rosaleen had no tales to tell and was full of home-coming.

"This kitchen is a disgrace," she said, putting things to rights. "But not for all the world would I live in the city, Dennis. It's a wild heartless place, full of criminals in every direction as far as the eye can reach. I was scared for my life the whole time. Light the lamp, will you?"

The native boy sat warming his great feet in the oven, and his teeth were chattering with something more than cold. He burst out: "I seed sumpin' comin' up the road whiles ago. Black. Fust it went on all fours like a dawg and then it riz and walked longside of me on its hind legs. I was scairt, I was. I said Shoo! at it, and it went out, like a lamp."

"Maybe it was a dog," said Dennis.

" 'Twarn't a dawg, neither," said the boy.

"Maybe 'twas a cat rising up to climb a fence," said Rosaleen.

" 'Twarn't a cat, neither," said the boy. " 'Twarn't nothin' I ever seed afore, nor *you*, neither."

"Never you mind about that," said Rosaleen. "I have seen it and many times, when I was a girl in Ireland. It's famous there, the way it comes in a black lump and rolls along the path before you, but if you call on the Holy Name and make the sign of the Cross, it flees away. Eat your supper now, and sleep here the night; ye can't go out by your lone and the Evil waiting for ye."

She bedded him down in Kevin's room, and kept Dennis awake all hours telling him about the ghosts she'd seen in Sligo. The trip to Boston seemed to have gone out of her mind entirely.

In the morning, the boy's starveling black dog rose up at the opened kitchen door and stared sorrowfully at his master. The cats streamed out in a body, and silently, intently they chased him far up the road. The boy stood on the doorstep and began to tremble again. "The old woman told me to git back fer supper," he said blankly. "Howma *ever* gointa git back fer supper *now?* The ole man'll skin me alive."

Rosaleen wrapped her green wool shawl around her head and shoulders. "I'll go along with ye and tell what happened," she said. "They'll never harm ye when they know the straight of it." For he was shaking with fright until his knees buckled under him. "He's away in his mind," she thought, with pity. "Why can't they see it and let him be in peace?"

The steady slope of the lane ran on for nearly a mile, then turned into a bumpy trail leading to a forlorn house with broken-down steps and a litter of rubbish around them. The boy hung back more and more, and stopped short when the haggard, long-toothed woman in the gray dress came out carrying a stick of stove wood. The woman stopped short too when she recognized Rosaleen, and a sly cold look came on her face.

"Good day," said Rosaleen. "Your boy saw a ghost last night, and I didn't have the heart to send him out in the darkness. He slept safe in my house."

The woman gave a sharp dry bark, like a fox. "Ghosts!" she said. "From all I hear, there's more than ghosts around your house nights, Missis O'Toole." She wagged her head and her faded tan hair flew in strings. "A pretty specimen you are, Missis O'Toole, with your old husband and the young boys in your house and the traveling salesmen and the drunkards lolling on your doorstep all hours—"

"Hold your tongue before your lad here," said Rosaleen, the back of her neck beginning to crinkle. She was so taken by surprise she couldn't find a ready answer, but stood in her tracks listening.

"A pretty sight you are, Missis O'Toole," said the woman, raising her thin voice somewhat, but speaking with deadly cold slowness. "With your trips away from your husband and your loud-colored dresses and your dyed hair—"

"May God strike you dead," said Rosaleen, raising her own voice suddenly, "if you say that of my hair! And for the rest may your evil tongue rot in your head with your teeth! I'll not waste words on ye! Here's your poor lad and may God pity him in your house, a blight on it! And if my own house is burnt over my head I'll know who did it!" She turned away and whirled back to call out, "May ye be ten years dying!"

"You can curse and swear, Missis O'Toole, but the whole countryside knows about you!" cried the other, brandishing her stick like a spear.

"Much good they'll get of it!" shouted Rosaleen, striding away in a roaring fury. "Dyed, is it?" She raised her clenched fist and shook it at the world. "Oh, the liar!" and her rage was like a drum beating time for her marching legs. What was happening these days that everybody she met had dirty minds and dirty tongues in their heads? Oh, why wasn't she strong enough to strangle them all at once? Her eyes were so hot she couldn't close her lids over them. She went on staring and walking, until almost before she knew it she came in sight of her own house, sitting like a hen quietly in a nest of snow She slowed down, her thumping heart eased a little, and she sat on a stone by the roadside to catch her breath and gather her wits before she must see Dennis. As she sat, it came to her that the Evil walking the roads at night in this place was the bitter lies people had been telling about her, who had been a good woman all this time when many another would have gone astray. It was no comfort now to remember all the times she might have done wrong and hadn't. What was the good if she was being scandalized all the same? That lad in Boston now—the little whelp. She spat on the frozen earth and wiped her mouth. Then she put her elbows on her knees and her head in her hands, and thought, "So that's the way it is here, is it? That's what my life has come to, I'm a woman of bad fame with the neighbors."

Dwelling on this strange thought, little by little she began to feel better. Jealousy, of course, that was it. "Ah, what wouldn't that poor thing give to have my hair?" and she patted it tenderly. From the beginning it had been so, the women were jealous, because the men were everywhere after her, as if it was her fault! Well, let them talk. Let them. She knew in her heart what she was, and Dennis knew, and that was enough.

"Life is a dream," she said aloud, in a soft easy melancholy. "It's a mere dream." The thought and the words pleased her, and she gazed with pleasure at the loosened stones of the wall across the road, dark brown, with the thin shining coat of ice on them, in a comfortable daze until her feet began to feel chilled.

"Let me not sit here and take my death at my early time of life," she cautioned herself, getting up and wrapping her shawl carefully around her. She was thinking how this sad countryside needed some young hearts in it, and how she wished Kevin would come back to laugh with her at that woman up the hill; with him, she could just laugh in their faces! That dream about Honora now, it hadn't come true at all. Maybe the dream about Kevin wasn't true either. If one dream failed on you it would be foolish to think another mightn't fail you too: wouldn't it, wouldn't it? She smiled at Dennis sitting by the stove.

"What did the native people have to say this morning?" he asked, trying to pretend it was nothing much to him what they said.

"Oh, we exchanged the compliments of the season," said Rosaleen. "There was no call for more." She went about singing; her heart felt light as a leaf and she couldn't have told why if she died for it. But she was a good woman and she'd show them she was going to be one to her last day. Ah, she'd show them, the low-minded things.

In the evening they settled down by the stove, Dennis cleaning and greasing his boots, Rosaleen with the long tablecloth she'd been working on for fifteen years. Dennis kept wondering what had happened in Boston, or where ever she had been. He knew he would never hear the straight of it, but he wanted Rosaleen's story about it. And there she sat mum, putting a lot of useless stitches in something she would never use, even if she ever finished it, which she would not.

"Dennis," she said after a while, "I don't put the respect on dreams I once did."

"That's maybe a good thing," said Dennis, cautiously. "And why don't you?"

"All day long I've been thinking Kevin isn't dead at

all, and we shall see him in this very house before long."

Dennis growled in his throat a little. "That's no sign at all," he said. And to show that he had a grudge against her he laid down his meerschaum pipe, stuffed his old briar and lit it instead. Rosaleen took no notice at all. Her embroidery had fallen on her knees and she was listening to the rattle and clatter of a buggy coming down the road, with Richards's voice roaring a song, "I've been working on the *railroad*, ALL the live-long day!" She stood up, taking hairpins out and putting them back, her hands trembling. Then she ran to the looking-glass and saw her face there, leaping into shapes fit to scare you. "Oh, Dennis," she cried out as if it was that thought had driven her out of her chair. "I forgot to buy a looking-glass, I forgot it altogether!"

"It's a good enough glass," repeated Dennis.

The buggy clattered at the gate, the song halted. Ah, he was coming in, surely! It flashed through her mind a woman would have a ruined life with such a man, it was courting death and danger to let him set foot over the threshold.

She stopped herself from running to the door, hand on the knob even before his knock should sound. Then the wheels creaked and ground again, the song started up; if he thought of stopping he changed his mind and went on, off on his career to the Saturday night dance in Winston, with his rapscallion cronies.

Rosaleen didn't know what to expect, then, and then: surely he couldn't be stopping? Ah, surely he *couldn't* be going on? She sat down again with her heart just nowhere, and took up the tablecloth, but for a long time she couldn't see the stitches. She was wondering what had become of her life; every day she had thought something great was going to happen, and it was all just straying from one terrible disappointment to another. Here in the lamplight sat Dennis and the cats, beyond in the darkness and snow lay Winston and New York and Boston, and beyond that were far off places full of life and gayety she'd never seen nor even heard of, and beyond everything like a green field with morning sun on it lay youth and Ireland as if they were something she had dreamed, or made up in a story. Ah, what was there to remember, or to look forward to now? Without thinking at all, she leaned over and put her head on Dennis's knee. "Whyever," she asked him, in an ordinary voice, "did ye marry a woman like me?"

"Mind you don't tip over in that chair now." said Dennis. "I knew well I could never do better." His bosom began to thaw and simmer. It was going to be all right with everything, he could see that.

She sat up and felt his sleeves carefully. "I want you

to wrap up warm this bitter weather, Dennis," she told him. "With two pairs of socks and the chest protector, for if anything happened to you, whatever would become of me in this world?"

"Let's not think of it," said Dennis, shuffling his feet.

"Let's not, then," said Rosaleen. "For I could cry if you crooked a finger at me."

The Cracked Looking-Glass

HACIENDA

Hacienda

IT was worth the price of a ticket to see Kennerly take possession of the railway train among a dark inferior people. Andreyev and I trailed without plan in the wake of his gigantic progress (he was a man of ordinary height merely, physically taller by a head, perhaps, than the nearest Indian; but his moral stature in this moment was beyond calculation) through the second-class coach into which we had climbed, in our haste, by mistake. . . . Now that the true revolution of blessed memory has come and gone in Mexico, the names of many things are changed, nearly always with the view to an appearance of heightened well-being for all creatures. So you cannot ride third-class no matter how poor or humble-spirited or miserly you may be. You may go second in cheerful disorder and sociability, or first in sober ease; or, if you like, you may at great price install yourself in the stately plush of the Pullman, isolated and envied as any successful General from the north. "Ah, it is beautiful as a *pulman!*" says the middle-class Mexican when he wishes truly to praise anything. . . . There was no Pullman with this train or we should most unavoidably have been in it. Kennerly traveled like that. He strode mightily through, waving his free arm, lunging his portfolio and leather bag, stiffening his nostrils as conspicuously as he could against the smell that "poured," he said, "simply poured like mildewed pea soup!" from the teeming clutter of wet infants and draggled turkeys and indignant baby pigs and food baskets and bundles of vegetables and bales and hampers of domestic goods, each little mountain of confusion yet drawn into a unit, from the midst of which its owners glanced up casually from dark pleased faces at the passing strangers. Their pleasure had nothing to do with us. They were pleased because, sitting still, without even the effort of beating a burro, they were on the point of being carried where they wished to go, accomplishing in an hour what would otherwise have been a day's hard journey, with all their households on their backs. . . . Almost nothing can disturb their quiet ecstasy when they are finally settled among their plunder, and the engine, mysteriously and powerfully animated, draws them lightly over the miles they have so often counted step by step. And they are not troubled by the noisy white man because, by now, they are accustomed to him. White men look all much alike to the Indians, and they had seen this maddened fellow with light eyes and leather-colored hair battling his way desperately through

their coach many times before. There is always one of
him on every train. They watch his performance with as
much attention as they can spare from their own always
absorbing business; he is a part of the scene of travel.

He turned in the door and motioned wildly at us
when we showed signs of stopping where we were.
"No, no!" he bellowed. "NO! Not here. This will never
do for you," he said, giving me a great look, protecting
me, a lady. I followed on, trying to reassure him by
noddings and hand-wavings. Andreyev came after, stepping tenderly over large objects and small beings, ex-
changing quick glances with many pairs of calm, lively
dark eyes.

The first-class coach was nicely swept, there were no
natives about to speak of, and most of the windows were
open. Kennerly hurled bags at the racks, jerked seat-
backs about rudely, and spread down topcoats and
scarves until, with great clamor, he had built us a nest
in which we might curl up facing each other, tempo-
rarily secure from the appalling situation of being three
quite superior persons of the intellectual caste of the
ruling race at large and practically defenseless in what
a country! Kennerly almost choked when he tried to
talk about it. It was for himself he built the nest, really:
he was certain of what he was. Andreyev and I were
included by courtesy: Andreyev was a Communist, and

Hacienda

I was a writer, or so Kennerly had been told. He had never heard of me until a week before, he had never known anyone who had, and it was really up to Andreyev, who had invited me on this trip, to look out for me. But Andreyev took everything calmly, was not suspicious, never asked questions, and had no sense of social responsibility whatever—not, at least, what Kennerly would ever call by such a name; so it was hopeless to expect anything from him.

I had already proved that I lacked something by arriving at the station first and buying my own ticket, having been warned by Kennerly to meet them at the first-class window, as they were arriving straight from another town. When he discovered this, he managed to fill me with shame and confusion. "You were to have been our guest," he told me bitterly, taking my ticket and handing it to the conductor as if I had appropriated it to my own use from his pocket, stripping me publicly of guesthood once for all, it seemed. Andreyev also rebuked me: "We none of us should throw away our money when Kennerly is so rich and charitable." Kennerly, tucking away his leather billfold, paused, glared blindly at Andreyev for a moment, jumped as if he had discovered that he was stabbed clean through, said, "Rich? Me, rich? What do you mean, rich?" and blustered for a moment, hoping that somehow the proper retort would emerge; but it would not. So he sulked for a moment, got up and shifted his bags, sat down, felt in all his pockets again to make certain of something, sat back and wanted to know if I had noticed that he carried his own bags. It was because he was tired of being gypped by these people. Every time he let a fellow carry his bags, he had a fight to the death in simple self-defense. Literally, in his whole life he had never run into such a set of bandits as these train porters. Besides, think of the risk of infection from their filthy paws on your luggage handles. It was just damned dangerous, if you asked him.

I was thinking that foreigners anywhere traveling were three or four kinds of phonograph records, and of them all I liked Kennerly's kind the least. Andreyev hardly ever looked at him out of his clear, square gray eyes, in which so many different kinds of feeling against Kennerly were mingled, the total expression had become a sort of exasperated patience. Settling back, he drew out a folder of photographs, scenes from the film they had been making all over the country, balanced them on his knees and began where he left off to talk about Russia. . . . Kennerly moved into his corner away from us and turned to the window as if he wished to avoid overhearing a private conversation. The sun was shining when we left Mexico City, but mile by mile through the solemn valley of the pyramids we climbed through the maguey fields towards the thunderous blue cloud banked solidly in the east, until it dissolved and received us gently in a pallid, silent rain. We hung our heads out of the window every time the train paused, raising false hopes in the hearts of the Indian women who ran along beside us, faces thrown back and arms stretching upward even after the train was moving away.

"Fresh pulque!" they urged mournfully, holding up their clay jars filled with thick gray-white liquor. "Fresh maguey worms!" they cried in despair above the clamor of the turning wheels, waving like nosegays the leaf bags, slimy and lumpy with the worms they had gathered one at a time from the cactus whose heart bleeds the honey water for the pulque. They ran along still hoping, their brown fingers holding the bags lightly by the very tips, ready to toss them if the travelers should change their minds and buy, even then, until the engine outran them, their voices floated away and they were left clustered together, a little knot of faded blue skirts and shawls, in the indifferent rain.

Kennerly opened three bottles of luke-warm bitter beer. "The water is filthy!" he said earnestly, taking a ponderous, gargling swig from his bottle. "Isn't it horrible, the things they eat and drink?" he asked, as if, no matter what we might in our madness (for he did not trust either of us) say, he already knew the one possible answer. He shuddered and for a moment could not swallow his lump of sweet American chocolate: "I have just come back," he told me, trying to account for his extreme sensitiveness in these matters, "from God's country," meaning to say California. He ripped open an orange trademarked in purple ink. "I'll simply have to get used to all this all over again. What a relief to eat fruit that isn't full of germs. I brought them all the way back with me." (I could fairly see him legging across the Sonora desert with a knapsack full of oranges.) "Have one. Anyhow it's clean."

Kennerly was very clean, too, a walking reproach to untidiness: washed, shaven, clipped, pressed, polished, smelling of soap, brisk and firm-looking in his hay-colored tweeds. So far as that goes, a fine figure of a man, with the proper thriftiness of a healthy animal. There was no fault to find with him in this. Some day I shall make a poem to kittens washing themselves in the mornings; to Indians scrubbing their clothes to rags and their bodies to sleekness, with great slabs of sweet-smelling strong soap and wisps of henequen fiber, in the shade of trees, along river banks at midday; to horses rolling sprawling snorting rubbing themselves against the grass to cleanse their healthy hides; to naked children shouting in pools; to hens singing in their dust baths; to sober fathers of families forgetting themselves in song under the discreet flood of tap-water; to birds on the boughs ruffling and oiling their feathers in delight; to girls and boys arranging themselves like baskets of fruit for each other: to all thriving creatures making themselves cleanly and comely to the greater glory of life. But Kennerly had gone astray somewhere: he had overdone it; he wore the harried air of a man on the edge of bankruptcy, keeping up an expensive establishment because he dared not retrench. His nerves were bundles of dried twigs, they jabbed his insides every time a thought stirred in his head, they kept his blank blue eyes fixed in a white stare. The muscles of his jaw jerked in continual helpless rage. Eight months spent as business manager for three Russian moving-picture men in Mexico had about finished him off, he told me, quite as though Andreyev, one of the three, were not present.

"Ah, he should have business-managed us through China and Mongolia," said Andreyev, to me, as if speaking of an absent Kennerly. "After that, Mexico could never disturb him."

"The altitude!" said Kennerly. "My heart skips every other beat. I can't sleep a wink!"

"There was no altitude at all in Tehuantepec," said

Andreyev, with stubborn gayety, "and you should have been there to see him."

Kennerly spewed up his afflictions like a child being sick.

"It's these Mexicans," he said as if it were an outrage to find them in Mexico. "They would drive any man crazy in no time. In Tehuantepec it was frightful." It would take him a week to tell the whole story; and, besides, he was keeping notes and was going to write a book about it some day; but "Just for example, they don't know the meaning of time and they have absolutely no regard for their word." They had to bribe every step of the way. Graft, bribe, graft, bribe it was from morning to night, anything from fifty pesos to the Wise Boys in the municipal councils to a bag of candy for a provincial mayor before they were even allowed to set up their cameras. The mosquitoes ate him alive. And with the bugs and cockroaches and the food and the heat and the water, everybody got sick: Stepanov, the camera-man, was sick; Andreyev was sick . . .

"Not seriously," said Andreyev.

The immortal Uspensky even got sick; and as for himself, Kennerly, he thought more than once he'd never live through it. Amoebic dysentery. You couldn't tell him. Why, it was a miracle they hadn't all died or had their throats cut. Why, it was worse than Africa. . . .

"Were you in Africa, too?" asked Andreyev. "Why do you always choose these inconvenient countries?"

Well, no, he had not been there, but he had friends who made a film among the pygmies and you wouldn't believe what they had gone through. As for him, Kennerly, give him pygmies or headhunters or cannibals outright, every time. At least you knew where you stood with them. Now take for example: they had lost ten thousand dollars flat by obeying the laws of the country —something nobody else does!—by passing their film of the Oaxaca earthquake before the board of censorship in Mexico City. Meanwhile, some unscrupulous native scoundrels who knew the ropes had beaten them to it and sent a complete newsreel to New York. It doesn't pay to have a conscience, but if you've got one what can you do about it? Just throw away your time and your money, that's all. He had written and protested to the censors, charging them with letting the Mexican film company get away with murder, accusing them of favoritism and deliberate malice in holding up the Russian film—everything, in a five-page typewritten letter. They hadn't even answered it. Now what can you do with people like that? Graft, bribe, bribe, graft, that's the way it went. Well, he had been learning, too.

"Whatever they ask for, I give 'em half the amount, straight across the board," he said. "I tell 'em, 'Look here, I'll give you just half that amount, and anything more than that is bribery and corruption, d'you understand?' Do they take it? Like a shot. Ha!"

His overwhelming unmodulated voice brayed on agonizingly, his staring eyes accused everything they looked upon. Crickle crackle went the dried twigs of his nerve ends at every slightest jog of memory, every present touch, every cold wind from the future. He talked on. . . . He was afraid of his brother-in-law, a violent prohibitionist who would be furious if he ever heard that Kennerly had gone back to drinking beer openly the minute he got out of California. In a way, his job was at stake, for his brother-in-law had raised most of the money among his friends for this expedition and might just fire him out, though how the fellow expected to get along without him Kennerly could not imagine. He was the best friend his brother-in-law had in the world. If the man could only realize it. Moreover, the friends would be soon, if they were not already, shouting to have some money back on their investment. Nobody but himself ever gave a thought to that side of the business! . . . He glared outright at Andreyev at this point.

Andreyev said: "I did not ask them to invest!"

Hacienda

Beer was the only thing Kennerly could trust—it was food and medicine and a thirst-quencher all in one, and everything else around him, fruit, meat, air, water, bread, were poisoned. . . . The picture was to have been finished in three months and now they'd been there eight months and God knew how much longer they'd have to go. He was afraid the picture would be a failure, now it hadn't been finished on time.

"What time?" asked Andreyev, as if he had made this answer many times before. "When it is finished it is finished."

"Yes, but it isn't merely enough to finish a job just when you please. The public must be prepared for it on the dot." He went on to explain that making good involves all sorts of mysterious interlocking schedules: it must be done by a certain date, it must be art, of course, that's taken for granted, and it must be a hit. Half the chance of making a hit depends upon having your stuff ready to go at the psychological moment. There are thousands of things to be thought of, and if they miss one point, bang goes everything! . . . He sighted along an imaginary rifle, pulled the trigger, and fell back exhausted. His whole life of effort and despair flickered like a film across his relaxed face, a life of putting things over in spite of hell, of keeping up a good front, of lying awake nights fuming with schemes and frothing with beer, rising of mornings gray-faced, stupefied, pushing himself under cold showers and filling himself up on hot coffee and slamming himself into a fight in which there are no rules and no referee and the antagonist is everywhere. "God," he said to me, "you don't know. But I'm going to write a book about it. . . ."

As he sat there, talking about his book, eating American chocolate bars and drinking his third bottle of beer, sleep took him suddenly, upright as he was, in the midst of a sentence. Assertion failed, sleep took him mercifully by the nape and quelled him. His body cradled itself in the tweed, the collar rose above his neck, his closed eyes and limp mouth looked ready to cry.

Andreyev went on showing me pictures from that part of the film they were making at the pulque hacienda. . . . They had chosen it carefully, he said; it was really an old-fashioned feudal estate with the right kind of architecture, no modern improvements to speak of, and with the purest type of peons. Naturally a pulque hacienda would be just such a place. Pulque-making had not changed from the beginning, since the time the first Indian set up a rawhide vat to ferment the liquor and pierced and hollowed the first gourd to draw with his mouth the juice from the heart of the maguey. Nothing had happened since, nothing could happen. Apparently there was no better way to make pulque. The whole thing, he said, was almost too good to be true. An old Spanish gentleman had revisited the hacienda after an absence of fifty years, and had gone about looking at everything with delight. "Nothing has changed," he said, "nothing at all!"

The camera had seen this unchanged world as a landscape with figures, but figures under a doom imposed by the landscape. The closed dark faces were full of instinctive suffering, without individual memory, or only the kind of memory animals may have, who when they feel the whip know they suffer but do not know why and cannot imagine a remedy. . . . Death in these pictures was a procession with lighted candles, love a matter of vague gravity, of clasped hands and two sculptured figures inclining towards each other. Even the figure of the Indian in his ragged loose white clothing, weathered and molded to his flat-hipped, narrow-waisted body, leaning between the horns of the maguey, his mouth to the gourd, his burro with the casks on either side waiting with hanging head for his load, had this formal traditional tragedy, beautiful and hollow. There were rows of girls, like dark statues walking, their mantles streaming from their smooth brows, water jars on their shoulders; women kneeling at washing stones, their blouses slipping from their shoulders—"so picturesque, all this," said Andreyev, "we shall be accused of dressing them up." The camera had caught and fixed in moments of violence and senseless excitement, of cruel living and tortured death, the almost ecstatic death-expectancy which is in the air of Mexico. The Mexican may know when the danger is real, or may not care whether the thrill is false or true, but strangers feel the acid of death in their bones whether or not any real danger is near them. It was this terror that Kennerly had translated into fear of food, water, and air around him. In the Indian the love of death had become a habit of the spirit. It had smoothed out and polished the faces to a repose so absolute it seemed studied, though studied for so long it was now held without effort; and in them all was a common memory of defeat. The pride of their bodily posture was the mere outward shade of passive, profound resistance; the lifted, arrogant features were a mockery of the servants who lived within.

We looked at many scenes from the life of the master's house, with the characters dressed in the fashion of 1898. They were quite perfect. One girl was especially clever. She was the typical Mexican mixed-blood beauty, her mask-like face powdered white, with a round hard full mouth, and hard slanting dark eyes. Her black waved hair was combed back from a low forehead, and she wore her balloon sleeves and small stiff sailor hat with marvelous elegance.

"But this must be an actress," I said.

"Oh, yes," said Andreyev, "the only one. For that rôle we needed an actress. That is Lolita. We found her at the Jewel Theater."

The story of Lolita and doña Julia was very gay. It had begun by being a very usual story about Lolita and don Genaro, the master of the pulque hacienda. Doña Julia, his wife, was furious with him for bringing a fancy woman into the house. She herself was modern, she said, very modern, she had no old-fashioned ideas at all, but she still considered that she was being insulted. On the contrary, don Genaro was very old-fashioned in his taste for ladies of the theater. He had thought he was being discreet, besides, and was truly apologetic when he was found out. But little doña Julia was fearfully jealous. She screamed and wept and made scenes at night, first. Then she began making don Genaro jealous with other men. So that the men grew very frightened of doña Julia and almost ran when they saw her. Imagine all the things that might happen! There was the picture to think of, after all. . . . And then doña Julia threatened to kill Lolita—to cut her throat, to stab her, to poison her. . . . Don Genaro simply ran away at this, and left everything in the air. He went up to the capital and stayed two days.

When he came back, the first sight that greeted his eyes was his wife and his mistress strolling, arms about each other's waists, on the upper terrace, while a whole scene was being delayed because Lolita would not leave doña Julia and get to work.

Don Genaro, who prided himself on his speed, was thunderstruck by the suddenness of this change. He had borne with his wife's scenes because he really respected her rights and privileges as a wife. A wife's first right is to be jealous and threaten to kill her husband's mistress. Lolita also had her definite prerogatives. Everything, until he left, had gone with automatic precision exactly as it should have. This was thoroughly outrageous. He could not get them separated, either. They continued to walk and talk on the terrace under the trees all morning, affectionately entwined, heads together, one a cinema Chinese—doña Julia loved Chinese dress made by a Hollywood costumer—the other in the stiff elegance of 1898. They remained oblivious to the summons from the embattled males: Uspensky calling for Lolita to get into the scene at once, don Genaro sending messages by an Indian boy that the master had returned and wished to see doña Julia on a matter of the utmost importance. . . .

The women still strolled, or sat on the edge of the fountain, whispering together, arms lying at ease about each other's waists, for all the world to see. When Lolita finally came down the steps and took her place in the scene, doña Julia sat nearby, making up her face by her round mirror in the blinding sunlight, getting in the way, smiling at Lolita whenever their eyes met. When they asked her to sit somewhere else, a little out of camera range, she pouted, moved three feet away, and said, "I want to be in this scene too, with Lolita."

Lolita's deep throaty voice cooed at doña Julia. She tossed strange glances at her from under her heavy eyelids, and when she mounted her horse, she forgot her rôle, and swung her leg over the saddle in a gesture unknown to ladies of 1898. . . . Doña Julia greeted her husband with soft affection, and don Genaro, who had no precedent whatever for a husband's conduct in such a situation, made a terrible scene, and pretended he was jealous of Betancourt, one of the Mexican advisers to Uspensky.

We turned over the pictures again, looked at some of them twice. In the fields, among the maguey, the Indian in his hopeless rags; in the hacienda house, theatrically luxurious persons, posed usually with a large chromo portrait of Porfirio Díaz looming from a gaudy frame on the walls. "That is to show," said Andreyev, "that all this really happened in the time of Díaz, and that all this," he tapped the pictures of the Indians, "has been swept away by the revolution. It was the first requirement of our agreement here." This without cracking a smile or meeting my eye. "We have, in spite of everything, arrived at the third part of our picture."

I wondered how they had managed it. They had arrived from California under a cloud as politically subversive characters. Wild rumor ran before them. It was said they had been invited by the government to make a picture. It was said they had not been so invited, but were being sponsored by Communists and various other shady organizations. The Mexican government was paying them heavily; Moscow was paying Mexico for the privilege of making the film: Uspensky was the most dangerous agent Moscow had ever sent on a mission; Moscow was on the point of repudiating him altogether, it was doubtful he would be allowed to return to Russia. He was not really a Communist at all, but a German spy. American Communists were paying for the film; the Mexican anti-government party was at heart in sympathy with Russia and had paid secretly an enormous sum to the Russians for a picture that would disgrace the present régime. The government officials themselves did not seem to know what was going on. They took all sides at once. A delegation of officials met the Russians at the boat and escorted them to jail. The jail was hot and uncomfortable. Uspensky, Andreyev, and Stepanov worried about their equipment, which was being turned over very thoroughly at the customs: and Kennerly worried about his reputation. Accustomed as he was to the clean, four-square business methods of God's own Hollywood, he trembled to think what he might be getting into. He had, so far as he had been able to see, helped to make all the arrangements before they left California. But he was no longer certain of anything. It was he who started the rumor that Uspensky was not a Party Member, and that one of the three was not even a Russian. He hoped this made the whole business sound more respectable. After a night of confusion another set of officials, more important than the first, arrived, all smiles, explanations and apologies, and set them free. Someone then started a rumor that the whole episode was invented for the sake of publicity.

The government officials still took no chance. They wanted to improve this opportunity to film a glorious history of Mexico, her wrongs and sufferings and her final triumph through the latest revolution; and the Russians found themselves surrounded and insulated from their material by the entire staff of professional propagandists, which had been put at their disposal for the duration of their visit. Dozens of helpful observers, art experts, photographers, literary talents, and travel guides swarmed about them to lead them aright, and to show them all the most beautiful, significant, and characteristic things in the national life and soul: if by chance anything not beautiful got in the way of the camera, there was a very instructed and sharp-eyed committee of censors whose duty it was to see that the scandal went no further than the cutting room.

"It has been astonishing," said Andreyev, "to see how devoted all of them are to art."

Kennerly stirred and muttered; he opened his eyes, closed them again. His head rolled uneasily.

"Wait. He is going to wake up," I whispered.

We sat still watching him.

"Maybe not yet," said Andreyev. "Everything," he added, "is pretty mixed up, and it's going to be worse."

We sat a few moments in silence, Andreyev still watching Kennerly impersonally.

"He would be something nice in a zoo," he said, with no particular malice, "but it is terrible to carry him around this way, all the time, without a cage." After a pause, he went on telling about Russia.

At the last station before we reached the hacienda, the Indian boy who was playing the leading rôle in the film came in looking for us. He entered as if on the stage, followed by several of his hero-worshipers, underfed, shabby youths, living happily in reflected glory. To be an actor in the cinema was enough for him to capture them utterly; but he was already famous in his village, being a pugilist and a good one. Bullfighting is a little out of fashion; pugilism is the newest and smartest thing, and a really ambitious young man of the sporting set will, if God sends him the strength, take to boxing rather than to bulls. Fame added to fame had given this boy a brilliant air of self-confidence and he approached us, brows drawn together, with the easy self-possession of a man of the world accustomed to boarding trains and meeting his friends.

But the pose would not hold. His face, from high cheekbones to square chin, from the full wide-lipped mouth to the low forehead, which had ordinarily the expression of professional-boxer histrionic ferocity, now broke up into a charming open look of simple, smiling excitement. He was happy to see Andreyev again, but there was something more: he had news worth hearing, and would be the first to tell us.

What a to-do there had been at the hacienda that morning! . . . Even while we were shaking hands all around, he broke out with it. "Justino—you remember Justino?—killed his sister. He shot her and ran to the mountains. Vicente—you know which one Vicente is?—chased him on horseback and brought him back." And now they had Justino in jail there in the village we were just leaving.

We were all as astounded and full of curiosity as he had hoped we would be. Yes, it had happened that very morning, at about ten o'clock. . . . No, nothing had gone wrong before that anyone knew about. No, Justino had not quarreled with anybody. No one had seen him do it. He had been in good humor all morning, working, making part of a scene on the set.

Neither Andreyev nor Kennerly spoke Spanish. The boy's words were in a jargon hard for me to understand, but I snatched key words and translated quickly as I could. Kennerly leaped up, white-eyed. . . .

"On the set? My God! We are ruined!"

"But why ruined? Why?"

"Her family will have a damage suit against us!"

The boy wanted to know what this meant.

"The law! the law!" groaned Kennerly. "They can collect money from us for the loss of their daughter. It can be blamed on us."

The boy was fairly baffled by this.

"He says he doesn't understand," I told Kennerly. "He says nobody ever heard of such a thing. He says

Justino was in his own house when it happened, and nobody, not even Justino, was to blame."

"Oh," said Kennerly. "Oh, I see. Well, let's hear the rest of it. If he wasn't on the set, it doesn't matter."

He collected himself at once and sat down.

"Yes, do sit down," said Andreyev softly, with a venomous look at Kennerly. The Indian boy seized upon the look, visibly turned it over in his mind, obviously suspected it to refer to him, and stood glancing from one to another, deep frowning eyes instantly on guard.

"Do sit down," said Andreyev, "and don't be giving them all sorts of strange notions not necessary to anybody's peace of mind."

He reached out a free hand and pulled the boy down to sit on the arm of the seat. The other lads had collected near the door.

"Tell us the rest," said Andreyev.

After a small pause, the boy melted and talked. Justino had gone to his hut for the noon meal. His sister was grinding corn for the tortillas, while he stood by waiting, throwing the pistol into the air and catching it. The pistol fired; shot her through here. . . . He touched his ribs level with his heart. . . . She fell forward on her face, over the grinding stone, dead. In no time at all a crowd came running from everywhere. Seeing what he had done, Justino ran, leaping like a crazy man, throwing away the pistol as he went, and struck through the maguey fields toward the mountains. His friend Vicente went after him on horseback, waving a gun and yelling: "Stop or I'll shoot!" and Justino yelled back: "Shoot! I don't care! . . ." But of course Vicente did not: he just galloped up and bashed Justino over the head with the gun butt, threw him across the saddle, and brought him back. Now he was in jail, but don Genaro was already in the village getting him out. Justino did not do it on purpose.

"This is going to hold up everything," said Kennerly. "Everything! It just means more time wasted."

"And that isn't all," said the boy. He smiled ambiguously, lowered his voice a little, put on an air of conspiracy and discretion, and said: "The actress is gone too. She has gone back to the capital. Three days ago."

"A quarrel with doña Julia?" asked Andreyev.

"No," said the boy, "it was with don Genaro she quarreled, after all."

The three of them laughed mightily together, and Andreyev said to me:

"You know that wild girl from the Jewel Theater."

The boy said: "It was because don Genaro was away on other business at a bad moment." He was being more discreet than ever.

Kennerly sat with his chin drawn in severely, almost

making faces at Andreyev and the boy in his efforts to hush them. Andreyev stared back at him in hardy innocence. The boy saw the look, again lapsed into perfect silence, and sat very haughtily on the seat arm, clenched fist posed on his thigh, his face turned partly away. As the train slowed down, he rose suddenly and dashed ahead of us.

When we swung down the high narrow steps he was already standing beside the mule car, greeting the two Indians who had come to meet us. His young hangers-on, waving their hats to us, set out to walk a shortcut across the maguey fields.

Kennerly was blustering about, handing bags to the Indians to store away in the small shabby mule car, arranging the party, settling all properly, myself between him and Andreyev, tucking my skirts around my knees with officious hands, to keep a thread of my garments from touching the no doubt infectious foreign things facing us.

The little mule dug its sharp hoof points into the stones and grass of the track, got a tolerable purchase at last on a cross tie, and set off at a finicking steady trot, the bells on its collar jingling like a tambourine.

We jogged away, crowded together facing each other three in a row, with bags under the seats, and the straw falling out of the cushions. The driver, craning around toward the mule now and then, and snapping the reins on its back, added his comments: An unlucky family. This was the second child to be killed by a brother. The mother was half dead with grief and Justino, a good boy, was in jail.

The big man sitting by him in striped riding trousers, his hat bound under his chin with red-tasseled cord, added that Justino was in for it now, God help him. But where did he get the pistol? He borrowed it from the firearms being used in the picture. It was true he was not supposed to touch the pistols, and there was his first mistake. He meant to put it back at once, but you know how a boy of sixteen loves to play with a pistol. Nobody would blame him. . . . The girl was nineteen years old. Her body had been sent already to the village to be buried. There was too much excitement over her; nothing was done so long as she was on the place. Don Genaro had gone, according to custom, to cross her hands, close her eyes, and light a candle beside her. Everything was done in order, they said piously, their eyes dancing with rich, enjoyable feelings. It is always regrettable and exciting when somebody you know gets into such dramatic trouble. Ah, we were alive under that deepening sky, jingling away through the yellow fields of blooming mustard with the pattern of spiked maguey shuttling as we passed, from straight lines to angles, to diamond shapes, and back again, miles and miles of it spreading away to the looming mountains.

"Surely they would not have had loaded pistols among those being used in the picture?" I asked, rather suddenly, of the big man with the red-tasseled cord on his hat.

He opened his mouth to say something and snapped it shut again. There was a pause. Nobody spoke. It was my turn to be uncomfortable under a quick exchange of glances between the others.

There was again the guarded watchful expression on the Indian faces. An awful silence settled over us.

Andreyev, who had been trying his Spanish boldly, said, "If I cannot talk, I can sing," and began in his big gay Russian voice: "Ay, Sandunga, Sandunga, Mamá, por Diós!" All the Indians shouted with joy and delight at the new thing his strange tongue made of the words. Andreyev laughed, too. This laughter was an invitation to their confidence. With a burst of song in Russian, the young pugilist threw himself in turn on the laughter of Andreyev. Everybody then seized the opportunity to laugh madly in fellowship, even Kennerly. Eyes met eyes through the guard of crinkled lids, and the little mule went without urging into a stiff-legged gallop.

A big rabbit leaped across the track, chased by lean hungry dogs. It was cracking the strings of its heart in flight; its eyes started from its head like crystal bubbles. "Run, rabbit, run!" I cried. "Run, dogs!" shouted the big Indian with the red cords on his hat, his love of a contest instantly aroused. He turned to me with his eyes blazing: "What will you bet, señorita?"

The hacienda lay before us, a monastery, a walled fortress, towered in terra cotta and coral, sheltered against the mountains. An old woman in a shawl opened the heavy double gate and we slid into the main corral. The upper windows in the near end were all alight. Stepanov stood on one balcony; Betancourt, on the next; and for a moment the celebrated Uspensky appeared with waving arms at a third. They called to us, even before they recognized us, glad to see anyone of their party returning from town to relieve the long monotony of the day which had been shattered by the accident and could not be gathered together again. Thin-boned horses with round sleek haunches, long rippling manes and tails were standing under saddle in the patio. Big polite dogs of expensive breeds came out to meet us and walked with dignity beside us up the broad shallow steps.

The room was cold. The round-shaded hanging lamp hardly disturbed the shadows. The doorways, of the style called Porfirian Gothic, in honor of the Díaz period of domestic architecture, soared towards the roof in a cloud of gilded stamped wallpaper, from an under·

growth of purple and red and orange plush armchairs fringed and tassled, set on bases with springs. Such spots as this, fitted up for casual visits, interrupted the chill gloom of the rooms marching by tens along the cloisters, now and again casting themselves around patios, gardens, pens for animals. A naked player-piano in light wood occupied one corner. Standing together here, we spoke again of the death of the girl, and Justino's troubles, and all our voices were vague with the vast incurable boredom which hung in the air of the place and settled around our heads clustered together.

Kennerly worried about the possible lawsuit.

"They know nothing about such things," Betancourt assured him. "Besides, it is not our fault."

The Russians were thinking about tomorrow. It was not only a great pity about the poor girl, but both she and her brother were working in the picture; the boy's rôle was important and everything must be halted until he should come back, or if he should never come back everything must be done all over again.

Betancourt, Mexican by birth, French-Spanish by blood, French by education, was completely at the mercy of an ideal of elegance and detachment perpetually at war with a kind of Mexican nationalism which afflicted him like an inherited weakness of the nervous system. Being trustworthy and of cultured taste it was his official duty to see that nothing hurtful to the national dignity got in the way of the foreign cameras. His ambiguous situation seemed to trouble him not at all. He was plainly happy and fulfilled for the first time in years. Beggars, the poor, the deformed, the old and ugly, trust Betancourt to wave them away. "I am sorry for everything," he said, lifting a narrow, pontifical hand, waving away vulgar human pity which always threatened, buzzing like a fly at the edges of his mind. "But when you consider"—he made an almost imperceptible inclination of his entire person in the general direction of the social point of view supposed to be represented by the Russians—"what her life would have been like in this place, it is much better that she is dead. . . ."

He had burning fanatic eyes and a small tremulous mouth. His bones were like reeds.

"It is a tragedy, but it happens too often," he said.

With his easy words the girl was dead indeed, anonymously entombed. . . .

Doña Julia came in silently, walking softly on her tiny feet in gay shoes like a Chinese woman's. She was probably twenty years old. Her black hair was sleeked to her round skull, eyes painted, apparently, in the waxed semblance of her face.

"We never really live here," she said, in a gentle smooth voice, glancing vaguely about her strange set-ting, in which she appeared to be an exotic speaking doll. "It's very ugly, but you must not mind that. It is hopeless to try keeping the place up. The Indians destroy everything with neglect. We stay here now for the excitement about the film. It is thrilling." Then she added, "It is sad about the poor girl. It makes every kind of trouble. It is sad about the poor brother. . . ." As we went towards the dining-room, she murmured along beside me, "It is sad . . . very sad . . . sad. . . ."

Don Genaro's grandfather, who had been described to me as a gentleman of the very oldest school, was absent on a prolonged visit. In no way did he approve of his granddaughter-in-law, who got herself up in a fashion unknown to the ladies of his day, a fashion very upsetting to a man of the world who had always known how to judge, grade, and separate women into their proper categories at a glance. A temporary association with such a young female as this he considered a part of every gentleman's education. Marriage was an altogether different matter. In his day, she would have had at best a career in the theater. He had been silenced but in no wise changed in his conviction by the sudden, astonishing marriage of his grandson, the sole inevitable heir, who was already acting as head of the house, accountable to no one. He did not understand the boy and he did not waste time trying. He had moved his furniture and his keepsakes and his person away, to the very farthest patio in the old garden, above the terraces to the south, where he lived in bleak dignity and loneliness, without hope and without philosophy, perhaps contemptuous of both, joining his family only at mealtimes. His place at the foot of the table was empty, the week-end crowds of sightseers were gone and our party barely occupied part of the upper end.

Uspensky sat in his monkey-suit of striped overalls, his face like a superhumanly enlightened monkey's now well overgrown with a simian beard.

He had a monkey attitude towards life, which amounted almost to a personal philosophy. It saved explanation, and threw off the kind of bores he could least bear with. He amused himself at the low theaters in the capital, flattering the Mexicans by declaring they really were the most obscene he had found in the whole world. He liked staging old Russian country comedies, all the players wearing Mexican dress, on the open roads in the afternoon. He would then shout his lines broadly and be in his best humor, prodding the rear of a patient burro, accustomed to grief and indignity, with a phallus-shaped gourd. "Ah, yes, I remember," he said gallantly, on meeting some southern women, "you are the ladies who are always being raped by those dreadful negroes!" But now he was fevered, restless, altogether silent, and his bawdy humor, which served as cover and disguise for all other moods, was gone.

Stepanov, a champion at tennis and polo, wore flannel tennis slacks and polo shirt. Betancourt wore well-cut riding trousers and puttees, not because he ever mounted a horse if he could avoid it, but he had learned in California, in 1921, that this was the correct costume for a moving-picture director: true, he was not yet a director, but he was assisting somewhat at the making of a film, and when in action, he always added a green-lined cork helmet, which completed some sort of precious illusion he cherished about himself. Andreyev's no-colored wool shirt was elbow to elbow with Kennerly's brash tweeds. I wore a knitted garment of the kind which always appears suitable for any other than the occasion on which it is being worn. Altogether, we provided a staggering contrast for doña Julia at the head of the table, a figure from a Hollywood comedy, in black satin pajamas adorned with rainbow-colored bands of silk, loose sleeves falling over her babyish hands with pointed scarlet finger ends.

"We mustn't wait for my husband," said doña Julia; "he is always so busy and always late."

"Always going at top speed," said Betancourt, pleasantly, "70 kilometers an hour at least, and never on time anywhere." He prided himself on his punctuality, and had theories about speed, its use and abuse. He loved to explain that man, if he had concentrated on his spiritual development, as he should have done, would never have needed to rely on mechanical aids to conquer time and space. In the meantime, he admitted that he himself, who could communicate telepathically with anyone he chose, and who had once levitated himself three feet from the ground by a simple act of the will, found a great deal of pleasurable stimulation in the control of machinery. I knew something about his pleasure in driving an automobile. He had for one thing a habit of stepping on the accelerator and bounding across tracks before approaching trains. Speed, he said, was "modern" and it was everyone's duty to be as modern as one's means allowed. I surmised from Betancourt's talk that don Genaro's wealth allowed him to be at least twice as modern as Betancourt. He could afford high-powered automobiles that simply frightened other drivers off the road before him; he was thinking of an airplane to cut distance between the hacienda and the capital; speed and lightness at great expense was his ideal. Nothing could move too fast for don Genaro, said Betancourt, whether a horse, a dog, a woman or something with metal machinery in it. Doña Julia smiled approvingly at what she considered praise of her husband and, by pleasant inference, of herself.

Hacienda

There came a violent commotion along the hall, at the door, in the room. The servants separated, fell back, rushed forward, scurried to draw out a chair, and don Genaro entered, wearing Mexican country riding dress, a gray buckskin jacket and tight gray trousers strapped under the boot. He was a tall, hard-bitten, blue-eyed young Spaniard, stringy-muscled, thin-lipped, graceful, and he was in a fury. This fury he expected us to sympathize with; he dismissed it long enough to greet everybody all around, then dropped into his chair beside his wife and burst forth, beating his fist on the table.

It seemed that the imbecile village judge refused to let him have Justino. It seemed there was some crazy law about criminal negligence. The law, the judge said, does not recognize accidents in the vulgar sense. There must always be careful inquiry based on suspicion of bad faith in those nearest the victim. Don Genaro gave an imitation of the imbecile judge showing off his legal knowledge. Floods, volcanic eruptions, revolutions, runaway horses, smallpox, train wrecks, street fights, all such things, the judge said, were acts of God. Personal shootings, no. A personal shooting must always be inquired into severely. "All that has nothing to do with this case, I told him," said don Genaro. "I told him, Justino is my peon, his family have lived for three hundred years on our hacienda, this is MY business. I know what hap-

258

pened and all about it, and you don't know anything and all you have to do with this is to let me have Justino back at once. I mean today, tomorrow will not do, I told him." It was no good. The judge wanted two thousand pesos to let Justino go. "Two thousand pesos!" shouted don Genaro, thumping on the table; "try to imagine that!"

"How ridiculous!" said his wife with comradely sympathy and a glittering smile. He glared at her for a second as if he did not recognize her. She gazed back, her eyes flickering, a tiny uncertain smile in the corners of her mouth where the rouge was beginning to melt. Furiously he ignored her, shook the pause off his shoulders and hurried on, turning as he talked, hot and blinded and baffled, to one and another of his audience. It was not the two thousand pesos, it was that he was sick of paying here, paying there, for the most absurd things; every time he turned around there at his elbow was some thievish politician holding out his paw. "Well. there's one thing to do. If I pay this judge there'll be no end to it. He'll go on arresting my peons every time one of them shows his face in the village. I'll go to Mexico and see Velarde. . . ."

Everybody agreed with him that Velarde was the man to see. He was the most powerful and successful revolutionist in Mexico. He owned two pulque haciendas which had fallen to his share when the great repartition of land had taken place. He operated also the largest dairy farm in the country, furnishing milk and butter and cheese to every charitable institution, orphans' home, insane asylum, reform school and workhouse in the country, and getting just twice the prices for them that any other dairy farm would have asked. He also owned a great aguacate hacienda; he controlled the army; he controlled a powerful bank; the president of the Republic made no appointments to any office without his advice. He fought counter-revolution and political corruption, daily upon the front pages of twenty newspapers he had bought for that very purpose. He employed thousands of peons. As an employer, he would understand what don Genaro was contending with. As an honest revolutionist, he would know how to handle that dirty, bribe-taking little judge. "I'll go to see Velarde," said don Genaro in a voice gone suddenly flat, as if he despaired or was too bored with the topic to keep it up any longer. He sat back and looked at his guests bleakly. Everyone said something, it did not matter what. The episode of the morning now seemed very far away and not worth thinking about.

Uspensky sneezed with his hands over his face. He had spent two early morning hours standing up to his middle in the cold water of the horse fountain, with